*"You are many things,
Melanie McFarlane, but weak
is not one of them."*

And then, because *he* was weak, he lowered his head and touched his lips to hers.

She didn't pull away. And when common sense finally penetrated the fog clouding Russ's brain and he listed his head, her eyes were no longer wet with tears.

Just a wary confusion that he recognized all too well. Because he felt the very same damn thing.

He lowered his hand and took a step back. Softly cleared his throat. "If we're gonna go, we'd better—"

"Give me t-ten minutes."

Russ nodded and backed toward the door. He felt as if he'd just run a marathon.

How the hell was he supposed to last for another five and a half months of this?

Dear Reader,

What is it about the Montana Mavericks that
we love so much? As a reader *and* a writer, I'm
thoroughly enamored of these larger-than-life
Western heroes and the strong, capable women
who capture their hearts. It is just pure fun to
wallow once again in the pages with them through
their laughter and their tears, and triumph along
with them when they find their happily-ever-after.

As for the hardheaded souls of this particular tale,
Russ and Melanie have differences that at first seem
insurmountable. But, of course, even with these two
who are so used to pushing others away, love finds
its way.

But isn't that one of the best things about love?

It finds a way.

All my best,

Allison Leigh

ALLISON LEIGH

A COWBOY UNDER HER TREE

Silhouette

SPECIAL EDITION

Published by Silhouette Books

America's Publisher of Contemporary Romance

Special thanks and acknowledgment are given
to Allison Leigh for her contribution to the
MONTANA MAVERICKS: STRIKING IT RICH series.

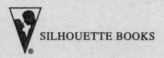 SILHOUETTE BOOKS

ISBN-13: 978-0-373-24869-8
ISBN-10:   0-373-24869-5

A COWBOY UNDER HER TREE

ALLISON LEIGH

started early by writing a Halloween play that her grade-school class performed. Since then, though her tastes have changed, her love for reading has not. And her writing appetite simply grows more voracious by the day.

She has been a finalist for the RITA® Award and Holt Medallion contests. But the true highlights of her day as a writer are when she receives word from a reader that she laughed, cried or lost a night's sleep while reading one of her books.

Born in Southern California, Allison has lived in several cities in four different states. She has been, at one time or another, a cosmetologist, a computer programmer and a secretary. She has recently begun writing full-time after spending nearly a decade as an administrative assistant for a busy neighborhood church. She currently makes her home in Arizona with her family. Allison loves to hear from her readers, who can write to her at P.O. Box 40772, Mesa, AZ 85274-0772.

This book is dedicated to my cohorts
in Striking It Rich crime: Christine Rimmer,
Stella Bagwell, Crystal Green, Pamela Toth,
and Victoria Pade, and our extraordinary editor,
Susan Litman, who keeps it all together.
It has been a pleasure and an honor
working with you.

Chapter One

"You want me to *what?*"

Melanie McFarlane's fingers tightened around the glass stem of her lemon-drop martini as she stared at the stupefied expression on Russ Chilton's annoyingly rugged face. "I believe you heard me." It took an enormous effort, but she kept her voice low. Mild. It helped that she had a lifetime of keeping herself well modulated and in control.

That's what one did, after all, when one was a McFarlane. Heaven forbid that they actually indulge in some sort of *human* manner.

"I heard you," Russ muttered. His long fingers were wrapped around the base of his beer bottle. No icy pilsner glass for him. He probably figured he was too salt-of-the-earth to bother with such niceties. "I just figured you're off your bean or something."

Or something, definitely. In her current vocabulary, *or something* was code for *increasingly desperate*.

She swallowed. Slowly turned the stem of her delicate martini glass and eyed the narrow twirl of lemon rind floating in the liquid. The waitress had already delivered their third round, and Melanie knew better than to finish off the drink when just two was already beyond her limit.

"It is important for me to make a success of this endeavor." She didn't believe it was any of his business just how important. Asking for his help in any way whatsoever was taking all of her strength as it was. Particularly when she knew he didn't approve of her presence in Thunder Canyon in the first place.

She didn't want anyone to know that it wasn't "McFarlane" money that was invested here. It was only Melanie's. And if she lost it all, she didn't know what she would do. Because returning to work for one of the McFarlane hotels wasn't an option for her.

Not anymore.

Russ snorted softly. "You mean you don't wanna fail at turning a perfectly good working ranch into some damn fool tourist trap. As if there aren't enough of those already cropping up around Thunder Canyon," he added derisively.

"The Hopping H will be a guest ranch," she corrected. "With your assistance, the actual—" her fingertips lifted "—ranch sort of activities will still continue." She was banking everything on Thunder Canyon's increasing popularity as a resort destination to help ensure her success. She knew plenty of people who would pay astronomical sums to get away from their high-pressure lives and at least play at getting back to what they thought of as "the simple life."

She'd been one of them, after all.

Only simple was turning out to be not quite so simple.

His lips twisted in a motion that *ought* to have made them look less sensual. "Ranch sort of activities," he mocked softly. "What's the matter, Red? Talking about shoveling manure and castrating calves a little too earthy sounding for you?"

Sadly, she had plenty of earthy thoughts where he was concerned, and not a single one of them were prudent.

Particularly for a McFarlane.

She needed this man's help, not his…his—

She managed to shut off the untoward thoughts as she softly cleared her throat and shifted in the hair-on-hide chair where they sat across from each other at a leather-topped table in the lounge at the Thunder Canyon Resort. The live band wasn't playing its usual eclectic mix, though, choosing instead to go with Christmas standards that were more in keeping with the holiday party that had been going on around them for the past few hours.

Melanie had never been a huge fan of the holidays, but just then, she felt even less than her usual smattering of holiday spirit. "I'm perfectly willing to shovel manure and do whatever as *well* as manage my guests' lodging and entertainment needs." She'd even learn how to cook and change bedding if she had to. And given her luck lately in holding on to ranching staff—well, *hands,* they were called—she just might need to.

He made a strangled sort of sound, as if he were trying not to choke. Or laugh.

This was not going the way she'd hoped.

Nothing about coming to Thunder Canyon was going the way she'd hoped. Scratch that. Even *before* she'd come to Thunder Canyon, nothing had gone the way she'd thought it would.

She was *supposed* to be in Atlanta, still capably running the newest jewel in the family crown—McFarlane House Atlanta. She would be, too, if she hadn't found out that while she'd been running things, her father and brother had been behind the scenes *really* calling the shots. She'd been nothing more than a figurehead. An ignorant, humiliated figurehead.

"Mr. Chilton—"

"Think you might as well call me Russ, ma'am." He leaned back in his high-backed bar stool, hooking an elbow behind him and looking every inch the poster boy for Western living.

Only there was nothing boyish about Russ Chilton.

From the tips of his leather boots—polished only because this was supposed to be a Christmas party, she suspected—up the six feet-plus of rangy muscle covered in black denim and thick Irish wool to the top of his dirty-blond hair that always seemed disheveled and an inch too long, he was a supremely well-grown male.

He wasn't handsome in the strictest sense. His nose was too hawkish, his jaw too square and stubborn.

But the end result was definitely good-looking.

But was he too good-looking for her peace of mind?

She needed someone believable, but she certainly didn't need someone she was in danger of falling for.

Fortunately for her, Russ Chilton could hardly stand her. So all she had to do was convince him they could help one another, and maybe she had a chance of success where the Hopping H was concerned.

"Fine." She sipped her drink, reminding herself that she was the one in control of this little tête-à-tête. "*Russ.* I know that you were interested in acquiring the Hopping H."

He sat forward suddenly, folding his elbows on the small high-top table, and seeming to take up all of her oxygen as he fairly loomed over her. "Interested?" There was no Western hospitality showing in his flinty brown eyes. "I had an offer in on the place with those city fools who inherited it from their grandparents, and you know it."

"And I beat your offer," she said reasonably. "It was simply a matter of business, Mr., er, Russ. It was nothing personal."

"Things in a town like Thunder Canyon *are* personal," he said evenly. "At least they always have been before—" His lips twisted again and he jerked his chin slightly, as if to encompass not only their surroundings, but the town beyond the walls of the Thunder Canyon Resort. "We don't need more progress," he said flatly. "We damn sure don't need more tourists to fill up the beds at your *guest* ranch. Go open a McFarlane House somewhere else, honey."

The "honey" was hardly an endearment. If anything, it was condescending, and her resolve stiffened. She didn't need condescension from anyone. She'd been living with plenty of it from her own family, thank you very much.

It was one of the things she hoped to put an end to

once and for all. All she needed was to turn the Hopping H into a success. A McFarlane-sized success.

Then maybe she'd finally get the respect she deserved.

"Progress is inevitable, Russ." Her teeth snapped off his name as it lingered on her tongue. "Which any intelligent person should recognize."

"Guess I'm just a dumb, backwoods hick, then." His drawl was deliberately thick. "Mebbe I should 'jess tip ma hat and thank ya for the opportunity of purrtendin' to be yer—"

"Shh. Keep your voice down. Please." She looked around them. Even at the late hour, there were plenty of partygoers still present, and she certainly didn't want someone overhearing. It had been foolish of her to bring up the subject with Russ at this time, anyway.

But she'd been watching him most of the evening as he worked through the crowd, seeming to be friendly with about half the guests. And then, when he'd been standing with his friend, Grant Clifton, who owned the original property she'd hoped to purchase, her thoughts had just seemed to finally coalesce.

Russ Chilton owned the Flying J, which bordered a sizable portion of the Hopping H.

He was her closest neighbor *and* he'd wanted the property for himself.

So she'd taken the bit between her teeth and run with it.

Just like her parents were always telling her—she'd obviously acted too hastily.

"What's the matter, Miz McFarlane?" His brown eyes hadn't warmed one iota. "If you'd wanted strict privacy for this discussion, you could have chosen a more discreet setting."

He was absolutely correct, of course. All he needed now was to tell her that she was behaving impetuously, and she'd suspect that Russ Chilton counted mind reading among his various talents. "Perhaps I thought you might be more approachable in a social setting." She turned the stem of her glass again. "A miscalculation on my part." She slid off the chair and gathered up her small red purse. "I'm sorry to have bothered you."

Her heart was in her throat as she turned to leave.

"Hold on there, Red."

Everything inside her sagged with relief but she knew that not a speck of that weakness showed on the outside. Thirty years of McFarlane existence had taught her that, at least.

She slowly turned on her heel, ignoring the way her head swam, and smoothed back a lock of her short hair that had fallen forward against her cheek. She gently lifted her eyebrows with inquiry. "Yes?"

"Is that look an acquired skill or a genetic trait?"

She tucked her slender purse beneath her arm, remaining silent.

He let out an aggravated breath. "Sit back down." He reached over and jerked her chair a few inches out from the table.

"Such gallantry." She slid back onto the high chair, slowly settling her purse in her lap. Outside the windows that overlooked the mountainside, the bright twinkly white lights seemed to dance more than usual. She blinked and focused instead on Russ's face.

It was not twinkly at all, and far more steady.

"Do I take it that you *are* interested in my offer, then?"

"Like you said. I'm interested in the Hopping H."

"Then we have an agreement." Act as if success were a foregone conclusion. Her parents had fed that to her along with her baby formula.

He lifted his hand. "Not so fast, sugar pie."

She wanted to shout with impatience. For six months now, ever since she'd stepped foot in Thunder Canyon, this particular man had been a thorn in her side. It was no wonder she'd needed an extra dose of Dutch courage to even approach him with her business proposition. "Is there something you'd like me to clarify?"

His lips twisted. "Oh, you've been pretty clear already."

"Then you can see that this arrangement is mutually beneficial. In return for your assistance, you'll receive a very generous interest in the Hopping H."

"Which only benefits me if *you* don't run the place into the ground."

"Which is *why* I need your assistance," she returned evenly. For pity's sake. How long would it take for the man to give his yea or nay? "You can ensure that never comes to pass by teaching me what I *do* need to know."

"What about your hired hands? Be an easier matter, I'd think, if you just learned about ranching business from the people you're already paying."

She studied his face, wondering if he were being sarcastic or not. Thunder Canyon was still, in many ways, a small community. And given her experience in the months she'd lived there, gossip was as much an avocation as skiing or hunting for gold. "My last two hands quit."

A faint flicker in his eyes warned her that maybe he truly hadn't known that fact. "Harlan and Danny?"

"Yes."

His lips tightened. "When?"

"Five days ago."

"And you've been staying on trying to manage everything on your own since then."

"Yes."

He made a noise under his breath that sounded like a rather creative oath. He gave her a square look that had her breath catching oddly in her throat. "I'm sorry. I didn't know."

She was grateful for the purse in her lap. It gave her fingertips something to dig into. "There's nothing for you to be sorry for," she assured smoothly. "It's not as if *you* were responsible it." The brothers who'd been her last remaining hands had simply quit with no notice whatsoever. They'd collected their final pay and had moved out of the bunkhouse by the end of the day. Where they'd gone, she had no clue.

Nor much care. They'd barely been better than no help at all.

"No wonder you're anxious for an answer," Russ was saying. "Look, Miz McFarlane—"

"Melanie. You have a mouthful of nicknames for me. Surely you can manage that. *Russ,*" she added pointedly.

He ignored her. "I don't know what kind of people you're used to, ma'am, but around here, neighbors tend to watch out for neighbors."

"Is that what you were doing three months ago when I moved onto the Hopping H and you assured me I was doomed to failure?"

"Pardon me for pointing out the obvious," he countered, "but you're sitting on land now with no hands on the payroll and judging by your offer to me—a desperate offer, I'll bet—not much of an idea how to manage on your own without them. Is that how you folks define success?"

Success was what being a McFarlane was all about.

She dropped the lemon rind from her unfinished drink on the small square napkin beneath the glass and tossed back the rest of the cocktail. "I'm looking for replacements for Harlan and Danny," she said. "But even when they *are* replaced—" the assurance was more bravado than anything since her efforts at hiring more hands had thus far been futile "—I want to know more about the ranch workings. I need to know." She leaned toward him, lowering her voice. "The Hopping H is my future, Mr. Chilton. As a working *guest* ranch. I am not going to let it fail. Either you can help me in that endeavor, and benefit quite nicely in the process, I might add, or I'll find someone else." She didn't know who, though. Hiring someone was out of the question, given the state of her finances. "Yes or no?"

"I get *half* an interest in the H."

"Yes." She'd thought about offering less, but desperate times called for desperate measures. And if—no, *once*—the guest ranch was on its feet and operating in the black, she'd be able to buy the man right back out again.

McFarlanes didn't "do" partnerships any more than they ever asked for help.

"And all I have to do is teach you enough about running a ranch so that you can keep your place from sinking under."

Her gaze darted around them. But nobody was

paying them any heed, particularly since the lavish midnight buffet was being set out. "Yes. That, and—"

His brows drew together in a mighty frown. "And do it all while pretending to be your husband," he finished.

Chapter Two

Russ watched the faint tide of red climb in Melanie McFarlane's lily-white cheeks at his flat summation.

"Yes," she replied in her slightly crisp voice. "That's the deal."

He picked up her empty martini glass and gave it an exaggerated sniff. "My old buddy Grant must be telling his barkeeps to pour heavy these days."

"I am not inebriated," she enunciated with the exaggeration of one who pretty much was. "Nor am I…off my bean, as you so eloquently phrased it."

"Nobody 'round here will believe we're hitched."

"Why not?"

He very nearly laughed out loud at that. "People know me, for one thing." And he'd made it more than plain that he had no intention of following the path to matrimony that every one of his buddies had been taking lately.

"Which means what? That you're not interested in women?"

"Not redheaded women with Boston in their vowels, that's for damn sure." Been there. Done that. Nobody who knew him would believe he'd repeat the experience.

"I've never lived in Boston," she assured snootily. "My family is from Philadelphia."

The moneyed part of it, he added silently, where he knew the headquarters of her family's hotel empire was located.

"And besides, the only people we need to convince of anything *are* my family," she continued.

"Why?"

She shook her head. "It doesn't matter. The point is, seduction is key."

"*What's* the key?"

"Discretion," she repeated so smoothly it left him wondering if he was the one who'd misheard, or she was the one who'd misspoke.

Either way, he damn sure needed to keep his mind off seduction where this woman was concerned. "What are you hoping to prove here, Melanie McFarlane?"

Her long lashes swept down, hiding her gaze. "I don't know what you mean. This is a business venture. Of course, I expect to succeed at it."

"Business ventures that involve you playacting as someone's wife. What's the deal? You'd rather have them think you're married to someone like *me,* than let them think you couldn't manage on your own?"

Her lashes flew up and he saw a tinge of guilt in her

expression. Enough to wonder if he hadn't hit on some truth. But all she did was turn up her nose a little in that way of hers. "I would be grateful if you could keep your voice down."

He wasn't exactly yelling. Hell. He didn't want any of his friends overhearing their conversation, either. At the rate that weddings and engagements were occurring around Thunder Canyon, God only knew what sort of rumors might be set into motion. "And you figure six months is all it'll take for you to learn the ins and outs of running the H." It was laughable, really. Either she thought he had superhuman abilities—which he doubted, given the uppity looks she usually gave him—or she had no clue what a huge bite she was trying to swallow.

"I should certainly understand the basics by then. At least enough to know whether my ranch hands are doing their jobs or not."

If Russ saw Harlan or Danny Quinn any time soon, he'd have a few words to say to the dolts. It wasn't as if hands didn't come and go. They did. But leaving a woman—no matter who she was—high and dry like they had was pretty damn low. "And if it's not enough time?"

She didn't look away. "Then naturally I would expect to renegotiate our agreement."

"You'd give me more than fifty percent?"

Her lips curved, revealing the perfect, gleaming white edge of her teeth. "I'm a businesswoman, Russ. What do you think? Not in this lifetime. But there could be some additional financial remuneration."

"You'd pay me cold hard cash to play your hus—"

She leaned forward, closing her hand over his forearm. "I believe we understand one another."

He understood that those long, slender fingers of hers might as well have been branding irons given the effect they had on his flesh. "Then understand this." He shifted and caught her hand in his as she went to draw away, and spotted the flicker in her deep brown eyes that she couldn't quite hide. "I may be just a rancher, ma'am. But I know how to smell cow patties when I see 'em."

She tugged at her hand and he loosened his grip enough for her to slowly work herself free. "You think this is some sort of game for me?"

"I don't know *what* this is for you," he admitted. "But there's no way in hell that I'd agree to this nonsense on just a handshake."

"I thought a man's handshake was his bond. Particularly in this part of the country."

"You're not from this part of the country."

She winced a little. "Are you suggesting that Easterners can't be trusted to keep their word?"

"Not the Easterners I've ever known. You want my help, then we get hitched for *real*. No pretense."

"But, but that's preposterous!"

"Is it?"

She sat back in her seat, brushing her fingers through her deep-red, lustrous hair. It fell back, perfectly, in its sleek lines against the nape of her long, elegant neck.

Even disconcerted, she looked as if she'd stepped off the cover of a fashion magazine. Not the faddish magazines filled with outlandish looks, but the expensive publications that only people of her ilk bothered to peruse.

Nola's kind of magazine.

"Don't worry," he added, brushing away thoughts of his ex-wife. "I'm not just trying to get into your pants."

The red that had risen in her cheeks drained away, leaving her looking pale, but no less stunning. "How reassuring." Her voice was thin.

Oh, yeah. He was the one who'd misheard.

She looked at him as if he were something to be scraped off the sole of her undoubtedly expensive hollyberry-red high heels.

"Unless that's what you're hoping for," he goaded.

"No," she assured hastily. "That is not on the table."

He looked at the high-top beneath their empty drinks. "You sure now? This here table looks mighty sturdy—"

"Are you naturally odious or is that an acquired skill?"

He very nearly laughed. As far as he was concerned, Melanie McFarlane was the epitome of high maintenance. She looked expensive. She talked expensive. She smelled expensive.

But she did keep his mind moving.

And God help him, he'd always been taken in by leggy redheads. Not this time, though. The last time he'd lost more than he could bear.

"Maybe I'm a bit of both," he allowed.

Her lips compressed.

The cocktail waitress appeared next to them, deposited a fresh round from her jam-packed tray and promised to return for the empties as soon as she could.

Melanie met his stare for an uncomfortable minute. Then she lifted her drink and gulped down half. She fiddled with her purse and drew out a slender gold pen, then pulled the fresh white napkin from beneath her drink. "I think your…idea…is overkill. Perhaps if we just put the terms in writing." She began writing carefully, then lifted her pen, looking at him as she slid the napkin toward him. "Does that make you feel better?"

He looked down at the list as he took a pull on his beer and wished he'd ordered a whiskey, instead. But then again, they'd both already had plenty to drink.

They *were* still sitting together at the table, after all. That had to be the result of alcohol. There was no other logical explanation.

The first several items on the napkin were straightforward, considering the nature of the agreement. Act as her husband—for the benefit of her family—and teach her everything she needed to know without *seeming* to teach her.

"Better?" He let out a disbelieving snort. "This is pretty damn crazy."

She didn't reply. Just wrapped those long, cool fingers of hers around her glass and sipped. If he wasn't mistaken, her hand wasn't entirely steady.

Nerves? Alcohol?

He pinched the bridge of his nose and looked at the napkin. After six months of their make-believe marriage, she would sign over fifty percent of the property to him.

Free and clear.

He could finally expand the Flying J into the Hopping H's prime territory. Not all of that territory, as he'd been planning to do for years, but half of it was nothing to sneeze at.

What was six months of his time, after all? He'd already put that, and more, into raising the funds to back his original offer on the H.

The offer that *she'd* trumped.

Now, he could have half the spread and plow his money back into it to boot.

From the corner of his vision, he watched her lift her drink again. Take a delicate sip. Set the glass carefully down.

She shifted slightly and the top of her red dress—a sort of wrapped thing that clung to her curves—gaped for a moment, giving him a fleeting glimpse of something pale and lacy against flesh that looked taut and full. It had to be his imagination that had him hearing the slide of her legs as she crossed one over the other. The bar was too damn noisy for him to have actually *heard* anything of the sort.

Imagination could be a pain in the ass.

He peered at her sloped handwriting, so cultured-looking and different than his own chicken scratching, as he reached the bottom of her stipulations.

"No hanky-panky," he read aloud, glancing up at her. She looked vaguely bored. But there was a thin line of white around her compressed lips that belied the demeanor. "It seemed prudent to add that point."

He figured the humor winding around inside him would be sort of misplaced just then. "I think my grandmother used to use that term." He leaned closer toward her, catching a whiff of her expensive scent. No imagination required there. Other than to wonder where she dotted that evocative perfume.

At the base of her neck? Her wrists? Between her breasts?

He stared into her eyes, making himself think of the Hopping H, and what he stood to gain. She'd said it herself.

This was business.

But seriously. *Hanky-panky?*

"I'm a rancher, babe," he said with the cocky wisdom of a ten-year-old poking a sleeping cat with a stick. "We call it by more basic terms."

Her eyes widened a little.

"Sex," he said wryly.

The relief that crossed her face was comical. Did she think he was so uncultured that he'd drop something *way* more basic?

Probably.

"Here's the deal." He set the napkin squarely in the center of the table, his palm covering her neat little list. "You can list your terms like this all you want. We can sign it. We can flippin' notarize it. Doesn't change the fact that I'm not *pretending* to be anything. Not for you. Not for anyone."

A swallow worked down her throat, drawing his eyes to the hollow at the base of it. Just below that seductive indentation, a single sparkling diamond seemed to almost float at the center of a nearly invisible chain. "Evidently, I misjudged the level of your interest in the Hopping H." She pinched her fingertips around the edge of the napkin. "I don't suppose I can prevail upon your holiday spirit to keep this discussion between the two of us?"

He kept his hand on the paper, preventing her from pulling it free. "People 'round here would tell you I don't have any holiday spirit."

She looked insulted. "I don't indulge in gossip, Mr. Chilton."

"What *do* you indulge in, Miz McFarlane?" Below

the sparkling diamond, there was another sweep of smooth, ivory skin, leading down to that wrapped dress.

She shifted in her seat, affording him another woefully brief glimpse of lace. "Quite obviously, wasting our time." She tugged at the napkin again.

"I didn't say you were wasting your time."

She let out a faint sigh. "Then what are you saying?"

"I told you. If we're going to do this, we're going to do this for real."

She leaned forward, the edges of her fine white teeth meeting in a smile that seemed remarkably close to a clench. "I am not looking for a *real* husband," she assured under her breath.

He leaned closer, too, mostly to see how quick she'd back away.

Only they ended up nose to nose, because the infernal woman didn't retreat.

"I'm not looking for a *real* wife, either," he murmured. Her skin was just as fine this close as his imagination suspected. And her lashes were long. Not the clumped-up, mucked-up kind of long that came out of some tube. He didn't kid himself that she went without cosmetics. Life with Nola had shown him just how effective that particular art could be. But he'd bet his favorite saddle that those lashes of Melanie's didn't have any need for artifice.

And those lashes suddenly flickered, dropping down to shield her dark eyes. "People are staring. Just give me the napkin and I'll go."

"Sugar, if you give up this easy, you might as well pack it in and move back to Boston." His fingers covered hers, stilling her tug on the napkin.

"I told you. I'm not from Boston and I'm *not* giving up."

"Then what would you call it?"

"Knowing enough not to beat a dead horse," she returned.

"Why don't you just sell me the H now, and cut your losses? Go back and run one of those towering hotels your family's famous for?"

"Why don't you just take a flying leap? Did you not just hear what I said? A McFarlane doesn't quit."

He smiled faintly. "Right. So if you don't want to fail, it's like I said. We get hitched for real. Then we'll have something to talk about."

"A person might think your virtue were at stake." Her voice was low and the smile on her lips didn't extend to her eyes.

His fingers itched to wrap around another beer. At least that was an easier explanation than thinking that his fingers itched to wrap around something much more warm and animated.

With hair the color of mahogany set on fire.

He curled the itchy fingers into a fist. "I gave up on virtue years ago. But I want to make damn sure you can't finagle your way out of giving me my cut when our little association ends."

"Aren't you two looking cozy?" The deep voice interrupted them.

Melanie's head whipped up, but Russ had to give her credit for her quick recovery. "Hello, Grant. Stephanie." Her smile for the couple was friendly. Warm. "Thank you again for inviting me to your party. It's a lovely way to kick off the season."

"We're glad you could make it," Steph assured. Her long blond hair was pulled back in a sparkly clip and her green eyes shined almost as much. "You, too, Russ."

Russ was watching the expression on Grant's face. Things had smoothed a lot between him and Grant in the past months, but they still hadn't quite gotten back to being as tight as they'd once been. Grant was Russ's oldest friend, but since Thunder Canyon had made the leap from being a bump in the road to the flavor of the year for the jet-setting crowd, they'd had more than a few differences.

Grant embraced the progress. He'd found a brand-new niche, managing the Thunder Canyon Resort. He fit in.

Russ didn't.

But at least Grant hadn't sold his family's ranch, Clifton's Pride, to the redhead, though. Of course, that had meant Russ lost out on the Hopping H when Melanie snapped it out from under *his* nose, instead.

"Yeah. Looks like you're doing plenty of celebrating." Grant's sharp blue eyes took in the collection of empty glasses and bottles on the table that the busy cocktail waitresses hadn't yet cleared away. "Why don't I set you both up with rooms tonight? We're almost at capacity, but there are a few cabins left."

"Worried about keeping the roads safe?" Russ drawled.

Grant smiled faintly. "Something like that. Cab service isn't exactly running swiftly tonight."

Russ eyed Melanie. "One room will do, won't it, darlin'?" No time like the present to start the townsfolk thinking that there *was* some hanky-panky going on between him and the Easterner.

He wasn't so far gone that he could turn down a

piece of the Hopping H. Business was business. She'd said so, herself.

Melanie swallowed again and slowly gave up her tug-of-war on the napkin. Her gaze—wide, brown, deep—focused on him. Her lips—soft, full, pink— parted softly. "One room is fine," she finally agreed, sounding oddly shy.

And just that quickly, Russ's damned imagination sidled into action again. His declaration had been pragmatic. His imagination was not.

Steph was doing a fair to middling job of hiding her shock. On the other hand, Grant didn't look all that shocked. Just knowing.

After all. He and Russ *did* go a long way back.

"I've already alerted the desk," his old friend said smoothly, proving one of the reasons why he was good at what he did. He anticipated things before they actually occurred. "You can pick up your key whenever you're ready."

Russ didn't look at Grant. He ran his fingertips deliberately over the back of Melanie's slender hand. Felt the tremble she couldn't hide. "Appreciate that."

"We'd better say good night to the Stevensons," Steph murmured to Grant. "Looks like they're getting ready to head out."

"Right." Grant covered the hand she tucked beneath his arm as if they'd been doing that all of their lives. "Catch you later." His lips twitched. "Enjoy yourselves, now."

"We plan to." Russ watched the color rise in Melanie's cheeks. "Supposed to snow sometime tonight, and the rooms here have outdoor hot tubs."

"You know what they're thinking," Melanie said under her breath once Grant and Steph moved off to intercept the departing couple.

"Exactly what you're wanting them to think," he returned. He lifted the beer bottle. Found it empty. Eyed her empty cocktail. "Want another round?"

"I think I've had plenty."

"Then we should hit the room. That is, if we've got a deal. A *real* deal."

She seemed to steel herself a little as she rose to her feet. She swept a shaking hand down the side of her dress and turned toward the door. "Bring the napkin."

"What for?" He caught her elbow in his hand, keeping her from sailing ahead of him as she looked prepared to do.

Her gaze swept down him from head to toe. The color in her cheeks bloomed even brighter. "Consider it a prenuptial agreement."

Chapter Three

Melanie simply had to shut off her brain as they went through the process of obtaining the offered room key and getting to their room, which was actually one of the cabins looking out over Thunder Canyon, rather than a single room in the lodge itself.

It felt as if she and the hunk of granite towering over her were the focus of every pair of eyes they passed, first at the registration desk, then the coat check where Russ almost mockingly tucked her into her calf-length fur. Nor was her ego healthy enough to believe that she would be the subject of any particular gossip. After six months, she was still a newcomer in Thunder Canyon.

A curiosity.

An oddity.

Russ, however, was as much a part of the town as the

foundation on which the charmingly Old West buildings were built. And it seemed very clear to her that he was definitely the focus of those curious looks.

They had to leave the main lodge to get to the cabin and the moment they stepped outside, Melanie felt the slap of cold, crisp air in her face.

It was both heady and sobering at the same time.

But she couldn't back down.

Which is why she soon found herself standing in the center of the small two-room cabin, facing a man who didn't like her, much less approve of her.

An electric hurricane-style lamp was already lit and it cast an intimate glow around the cabin. The interior looked rustic without being rustic and despite the haze clouding her sensibilities, her McFarlane brain still managed to take in the amenities of the cabin.

Pure luxury.

Similar to what she hoped to offer *her* guests.

She jerked a little when Russ dropped the cabin key on the long pine table surrounded by four chairs in the dining area. Seeming oblivious to her, he shrugged out of his shearling coat and tossed it onto the leather couch that was draped with a red-and-black-plaid woolen throw. There were also two comfortable-looking armchairs and an enormous ottoman that doubled as a coffee table. He brushed past her, entering the small, efficient kitchen area. "Take off your coat."

Evidently, his helping her into it had been for the benefit of the people watching them. She set her purse on the table and slid off the mink that her father had given her for her twenty-fifth birthday and draped it carefully over one of the ladder-back chairs.

She tried to see through the open doorway that led to the bedroom, but it was too dark.

She heard him rummaging in a cupboard and was surprised when he returned to the table without another drink from what she expected would be a well-stocked bar.

Instead, he had a ballpoint pen in his hand. He yanked out a chair, sat down, and tossed the somewhat crumpled napkin on the table in front of him. He clicked the end of the pen and added his own scrawl beneath hers.

When he finished, his dark gaze was brooding as he slid the napkin across the smooth wooden surface toward her. "You gonna stand there all night, or sit yourself down?"

"Stand." She picked up the napkin and read his additions, under which he'd confidently signed his name. Russ J. Chilton.

"It's not short for Russell?"

He just watched her.

What did it matter what his name was? She tossed the ink-riddled napkin back to him. His first term had been that their marriage be performed legally. He'd already made that point perfectly clear. The second was the description of acreage he wanted when it came to getting his division of the Hopping H. But the last condition?

She gave him a look. "I need you to teach me what I need to know, not agree to do everything *you* tell me to do."

"Where the Hopping H is concerned," he pointed out the rest of his statement with a shrug. "Someone's gotta be the boss."

"And I suppose where you're concerned that'll never be a woman." She managed not to roll her eyes.

"It won't be a woman who doesn't know the front end of a horse from the back."

Then she did roll her eyes. "And women are accused of exaggeration. Believe me, Mr. Chilton, I know which end is which, and currently, you're acting like the hind end."

He shrugged again, obviously unfazed. "You can do all the bossing you want when it comes to your guest enterprise." His lips twisted at that, telling her yet again what he thought of that particular endeavor. "But when it comes to ranch operations, I call the shots. Or there's no deal. You can go find yourself some other sucker."

"I'm not looking for any kind of sucker. Just someone who'll give me a fair deal and exercise some discretion at the same time."

"And you think that you'll get that from me."

She lifted an eyebrow. "Won't I?"

"You don't know anything about me."

She unfolded her arms and closed her hands over the back of the mink-draped chair. It seemed to help the way the room tended to spin around her head. She really shouldn't have had that last martini. "We don't have to like one another to acknowledge certain facts. And one is that you're scupu…scrupulously fair. Everyone in town says so."

He made a soft grunt. "Too damn fair. What's your family got to do with all of this?" He shoved his hand through his hair, leaving it even more rumpled.

Probably what he looked like when he woke in the morning.

She swallowed, trying to banish the thought. "Hmm?"

"You said only your family had to believe we were married. Why?"

Her fingers sank farther into the fur. "They need to believe I'm competent in all areas of the guest ranch. Being married is a side note to them. Why would you trust getting your share out of a marriage—an uncostumated…consummated marriage—more than you'd trust a contract?"

His gaze seemed to drop to her lips. "Does it matter?"

Touché. She leaned over the table and slid the pen from between his fingers. Before she could talk herself out of it, she signed her name with a flourish, right beneath his.

Then she tossed the pen on the table and straightened. The bravado had a price, though, and it was called *head rush.* She gripped the back of the chair again, waiting until her vision cleared and the room stopped swaying. "I'll make arrangements, then, for this *legal* marriage."

"No. I'll do it."

"What's wrong? Don't you trust me?"

He unfolded himself from the chair and smiled humorlessly as he very deliberately picked up the napkin, folded it in half and tucked it in his back pocket. "I shouldn't have trusted the last woman I married. Why would you be any different?"

Leaving Melanie blinking at that, he headed through the cozy living area and into the darkened bedroom beyond. A moment later, a soft light came on and she saw the foot of an enormous lodgepole bed.

One bed.

Naturally.

Russ was out of her line of sight, but a familiar-looking ivory sweater was tossed onto the foot of that bed.

She chewed her lip and looked sideways at the leather couch.

"If you were any sort of gentleman, you'd offer to take the couch," she said loudly enough for him to hear.

"Being fair doesn't mean being a gentleman." He appeared in the doorway and Melanie nearly wilted with relief that beneath his sweater he'd worn a white T-shirt.

A white T-shirt that clung faithfully to every line of his impossibly wide chest.

She barely had time to brace herself for the bed pillow that he tossed across the room to her.

"They keep extra blankets in that hassock thing," he told her. "Lid lifts up and they're inside. Get some sleep. We've got a busy day ahead of us."

Then he turned his back on her and closed the door between them.

Melanie squeezed the downy pillow between her hands.

She wasn't sure if she were envisioning his neck or not.

She turned to the couch and tossed the pillow on it. The ottoman did, indeed, contain storage beneath the heavy leather-topped lid and she pulled out two blankets, which she spread out on the couch.

Eyeing the closed bedroom door, she nibbled her lip as she stepped out of her high heels. She needed the restroom. And not just to clean her face and her teeth. But she'd rather go out into the cold night and hide behind some bush rather than knock on that door.

The door that suddenly opened, as if the man behind it had, once again, been reading her mind. "Bathroom's free," he said abruptly.

The T-shirt was gone.

She dragged her eyes away from the dusty brown hair swirling across his chest and arrowing down a ridged abdomen that *should* have been winter pale, but wasn't.

The last man she'd occasionally dated in Atlanta had been exactly six-one, worked out two hours a day, ran marathons and religiously waxed his chest. He'd been more beautiful than most women, utterly sophisticated and, amazingly enough, he'd been straight.

But for some ungodly reason, the appeal of Russ's masculinity soared to a universe far beyond Michael's. She'd never once contemplated becoming intimate with Michael, any more than she'd considered it with any of the other men who'd escorted her over the years.

That was, until she'd met *this* irritating man.

Now, she seemed to struggle with those unfamiliar thoughts every time she turned around and she knew if *he* knew that she'd managed to attain the age of thirty without sleeping with a man, he'd have a field day with the knowledge.

She was five-seven, but she still wished she hadn't been so quick to remove her shoes as she sailed past Russ and all his appallingly glorious muscle and flesh into the spacious bathroom beyond the king-size bed, because he seemed larger than ever.

She closed the door and leaned back against it, stupidly feeling as if she needed to catch her breath. As if she'd just run some sort of gauntlet.

It was so ridiculous. Melanie didn't *get* breathless over men, much less men who figured she wasn't worth the time of day.

A mirror across from the door reflected her image and she stared hard at herself. Made herself remember just what she was working to accomplish here.

It had *nothing* to do with personal relationships, and everything to do with business.

That was who she was.

She let out a long breath. Ran her hand through her hair and straightened deliberately from the door. She was merely overreacting to the stress of the situation.

That was all.

Feeling more like herself, she reached for one of the twin robes that were provided by the resort. The shower was separate from the oversize, jetted tub and she turned it on, letting the rushing sound of water continue the job of soothing her jagged nerves. Moving more quickly than her swimming head was comfortable with earned her a stubbed toe and soap in her eyes when she washed her face. There were small complimentary tubes of toothpaste but no toothbrushes, and as she made do with a nubby washcloth and her finger to do the job, she vowed that the Hopping H would not be remiss in that area.

On the other hand, the soaps and lotions provided were about as heavenly as anything that McFarlane House hotels had ever provided. Showered and clean, she tossed aside the towel and folded herself into the smaller of the two thick terry robes. She rinsed out her lingerie and commandeered the robe hangers for them and her dress which she hung on the back of the bathroom door and opened it again, and acting as if she had blinders on, tossed the larger robe in the general direction of the bed as she strode back out to the living area.

Only Russ was stretched out on the couch, his ankles propped on one arm, his head on the other. He'd dragged one of the soft blankets halfway up his chest. One hand hung off the couch, propped on the ottoman. His other was thrown over his head.

Sound asleep.

She pressed her lips together, thoroughly disconcerted.

"Go before I change my mind," he muttered softly.

Not sound asleep, she quickly revised.

She turned on her bare heel and fled back into the bedroom, softly closing the door behind her.

His ivory sweater was still in a heap on the foot of the bed. Feeling very odd about it, she picked it up, laying it out over the bare pine dresser top.

His T-shirt was on the floor and she gave it a wide berth as she pulled back the thick red comforter that topped the bed. The linens were crisp and fresh when she climbed between them and sighing, she sank into the downy pillows.

By all rights, exhaustion and alcohol should have assured her of immediate sleep.

So, naturally, the moment she turned off the lamp next to the bed, all she did was stare, wide-eyed, into the darkness.

Dawn had barely broken when Russ gave up trying to sleep.

He tossed back the blanket and sat up on the couch,

shoving his hands through his hair, pressing the heels of his palms into his eye sockets.

He ought to be following his own advice of getting some sleep.

Too bad every time he'd closed his eyes, his imagination had gone into torture mode.

Probably what he got for trading six months of so-called marriage for a hunk of land that he'd been wanting ever since he'd assumed control of the Flying J after his dad died. Jasper Chilton had been more than happy to keep the Flying J just as it had been when *he'd* taken it over from his father.

But not Russ.

Hell, no. *He* had to want more, and look where it had landed him.

Promising to marry a woman no more suitable for him than Nola had been.

At least this time his eyes were wide-open. He was more than a decade older than the twenty-one-year-old kid he'd been back then, and no ridiculous notions of love were clouding his brain these days. Who knew what would happen? Maybe the next six months would be far less torturous than the two years of wedded "bliss" that he and Nola had shared before she'd permanently hared off back to the bosom of her Bostonian family.

Most importantly, this time he'd be able to keep what he wanted out of the deal.

Half of the Hopping H was a poor comparison for the loss of the son he never saw anymore, but it was the only positive note on the horizon as far as Russ could see.

So he'd take what he could get.

Even if it meant playing house for a while with Melanie McFarlane.

He pushed off the couch and found coffee makings in the kitchen, probably taking too much pleasure in the noise he was making while he was about it. But if *she* wanted to know more what ranching life was supposed to be about, she'd damn sure better get used to rising with the chickens.

He'd built himself up a fine head of steam about the matter by the time the coffeepot was half full. He yanked out the pot, stuck his mug beneath the steaming stream from the coffeemaker until it was full, then stuck the pot back in place. Feeling stifled inside the cozy cabin, he shoved open the wide door that led out onto the wraparound-style porch and went outside, mug in hand.

The cold doused him from bare feet to bare head, and he let out a long sigh.

As far as his eye could see were signs that Thunder Canyon would never again be the hometown where he'd grown up. There were more schools. More shopping centers. More this. More that.

Even now, despite the early hour, he could see the dots of people working their way along the ski slopes even though the lift wasn't yet running. From one of the resort's restaurants—probably the Grubstake—he could already smell the scent of frying bacon.

His stomach rumbled.

Too many beers last night and not enough food.

Another thing that would be easy to blame on *her.*

Only his parents hadn't raised him to shuck off his

own responsibilities. Melanie hadn't held a gun to his head.

He'd jumped without a parachute after the carrot she'd dangled all on his own.

"Good Lord. Have you lost your mind? It's freezing out there."

He looked over his shoulder at her. "Well, well. If it isn't the future Mrs. Chilton."

Her lips turned down at the corners. "I don't recall agreeing to change my name."

He actually hadn't expected otherwise, but why let her know that? "There ain't no staff people hanging around here to serve you coffee."

Her eyes with those thick dark lashes narrowed. Her hair was slightly rumpled and she was bundled to her chin in the massive red blanket from the bed. It ought to have clashed with her auburn hair—he'd learned such things thanks to Nola's clotheshorse ways—but it didn't. If anything, Melanie looked...too damned tasty.

Soft. Sleepy. Female.

And everything inside him stirred annoyingly to life.

He looked away at the snowy mountainside. Cold was definitely a good thing. "You want some, get it yourself. It's hot in the kitchen," he finished.

"I don't drink coffee." Her voice was snooty again. "And you're letting in all the cold air."

He didn't look back at the rustle of bedding that preceded the not-so-soft slam of the door. He pulled out the napkin from his back pocket and squinted at the splotchy lines of writing they'd made on it the night before. In the cold sober morning light, his signature was even more of a scrawl than usual, and her neat penmanship showed some decided unevenness.

No hanky-panky.

She'd even underlined it. Twice.

Muttering an oath not only at himself but at the universe in general, he tucked the napkin back in his pocket, then leaned his forearms on the rail of the deck and glared at the million-dollar view.

"Happy wedding day, Russ," he muttered under his breath. "Welcome back to hell."

Chapter Four

Melanie *would* have liked to have locked that door between her and Russ J. Chilton, leaving him stewing out there in the frigid air.

But a frozen stick of ice wasn't going to be able to teach her what she needed to know to keep the Hopping H from falling apart before she could even open its first guest cabin. So she kept her itchy fingers from flipping the lock and returned to the bedroom where she *did* lock the door.

Not that he'd be likely to break it down anytime soon. The man couldn't be clearer where his distaste for her was concerned. She hoped he would manage to get that under some control, at least when they were around other people.

She washed up, touching her lips with some gloss

from her small purse and dashing her comb through her hair, then pulled on her dress from the night before, wrinkling her nose a little at the smell of cigarette smoke that clung to the fabric. Unfortunately, her bra and panties were still damp and since Russ was still out on the porch when she left the bedroom, she quickly shoved them into the deep side pocket of her mink. Then she pulled on the coat, pushed her bare feet into her shoes, and yanked open the door again.

He was leaning over, elbows bent atop the rail, displaying those ridiculously wide, bare shoulders again, and—drat it all—a very fine denim-covered rear.

She wished she'd worn her panties and bra after all, damp or not. Because even if *he* didn't know she didn't have a stitch on beneath her dress, she did. "Are you going to lollygag there all day, or what?"

He sent her a slow look over his bare shoulder that had an annoying jolt curling low through her abdomen. "Anxious to find a justice of the peace, are you?"

She flipped up the collar of her coat, holding it closely together beneath her chin. "I'd like to go home and change first. But, yes, the sooner we start, the sooner you'll be the proud owner of more land."

"And we'll be free of each other."

"Exactly."

He straightened and walked past her, leaning his head close to hers as he went. "We're just a match made in heaven," he murmured.

She managed to hold her ground. "At least we both know what we want out of the deal," she returned as he came inside.

She was waiting by the door, purse in hand, when

he came back out of the bedroom a short time later, his hair damp and slicked back from his face, and his naked chest once more hidden beneath that thick ivory wool. "I cleaned out the coffeemaker," she told him before he went into the kitchen, presumably to take care of the matter himself.

"Without breaking a fingernail?" He grabbed his coat but didn't bother to pull it on. "Someone should give you an award."

"This will be considerably easier if you could stow your foul humor for a while."

"Afraid I can't act the lovesick fool who'd toss aside all rhyme and reason to get married again?" He nudged her through the door and closed it behind him, checking that it was locked.

"Considering how you talk about it, one might think you're still in love with your former wife."

He snorted and headed down the steps to the snow-plowed sidewalk that led back toward the main lodge. "Right. Watch the path there. Looks like some ice."

She avoided the spot he pointed at, hurrying to keep up with his long strides. "How long ago was it?"

"What business is it of yours?"

"We're supposed to be getting married," she reminded. "Presumably these are things that we would want to know about one another. If, you know, if the situation were *real*."

"Well, it isn't." He continued striding ahead of her.

She strongly considered sticking her tongue out at the back of his head, but curtailed the childish impulse. She was a thirty-year-old hotelier, not a spoiled heiress the way he seemed to want to think.

By the time she caught up to him inside the resort, he was turning in the cabin key. She went out the front where she'd left her car parked the night before and pulled her car keys from her purse as she waited for him.

"I'll take those." He went to pluck the keys from her fingertips, and she jerked them away.

"I beg your pardon?"

"It's a husband's job to drive."

She let out a disbelieving laugh. "Oh, please." But when Russ held out his palm, clearly in demand, she shoved the keys in her coat pocket. "You're not driving my car. You won't even *fit* in my car. We can just meet back at the Hopping H."

"Don't think so." Before she knew it, he'd reached into her coat pocket and extracted the keys.

Along with her panties.

She wanted the ground to swallow her whole.

"Well, well." He let the panties hang from his index finger. "Unless you're carrying a spare—"

She snatched them off his finger and shoved them back into her pocket. "You're making a scene."

"Hey, babe, I'm just trying to drive us to the chapel."

"Fine. You want to drive? Drive." She ignored his goading smile.

"That's yours over by the tree, right?"

She knew good and well that he recognized her sports car, because he'd made a point several months earlier of telling her that such a vehicle was useless on a ranch. "Are you going to play caveman from here on out, or act like a civilized human being?"

"Don't know." He crossed the parking lot and

managed to press the correct buttons on her remote to unlock the car without setting off the alarm. "If I feel a yen to throw you over my shoulder and start brandishing a big wooden club, I'll let you know. But at least I keep my drawers on," he added. "Seems the mark of a civilized man."

Humiliated, she yanked open the passenger door when it became embarrassingly apparent that he wasn't going to open her door for her and slid inside. She knew he'd have to adjust the driver's seat to his height, and she resolutely remained silent. He could figure it out for himself. When he knocked his knee into the steering column in the process, she smiled innocently. "What about your vehicle?" She didn't see the ramshackle truck she'd seen him driving around town parked in the lot.

"What about it?"

She exhaled slowly. Undoubtedly, his orneriness was another attempt to get under her skin. "Just so you know," she told him evenly, "you can do all the driving you want, but *I* am not doing your laundry."

He gave a sudden bark of laughter. "Do you even know what the washing machine looks like?"

She lifted her nose into the air and looked out the side window. What was it to him if she'd had to read the directions in the owner's manual…twice? It wasn't *her* fault that she'd been raised in a setting that ensured such matters had always been taken care of by someone else.

Being a McFarlane hadn't been about how well she could play at household chores. It was about how well she could manage a luxury hotel.

And she'd *thought* she'd been doing an admirable job of it, until she'd learned otherwise.

She pressed her palms together. Now that the decision had been made to actually *get* married, she wasn't certain how to proceed. "Do you, um, know what the marriage license requirements are in Montana? Blood tests? Waiting period? Anything?"

"Don't know."

"So you didn't get married here, before?"

His gaze slid her way for a moment before he zoomed out of the parking lot with more finesse than she'd have expected for a man who didn't seem to drive anything but ancient, rattling pickup trucks. "Nope."

She refused to indulge her curiosity. "I guess we can wait until Monday to find out."

"We'll fly to Vegas this afternoon."

"So soon?"

"Cold feet already?" His voice was mocking.

"Of course not." But her stomach muscles were clenching. Which was ridiculous. The only difference between the proposition she'd made to him and the final agreement they'd come to was a license. A piece of paper. What did it matter if that paper was signed now or five days from now?

They made the rest of the drive to the Hopping H in silence. He parked in front of the wide stone steps that led up to the main house. "Pack light," he ordered. "I'm gonna check the barn and the stock."

She hadn't needed the reminder of where his priorities were but it was probably just as well.

She went up the steps that had already undergone significant repair and restoration and unlocked the door.

She looked back, watching him continue driving along the gravel road that eventually would lead him to the Hopping H's outbuildings. Lord only knew what sort of comments she'd earn once he'd assessed the situation there.

Her gaze skipped over the tall snow-heavy pines that surrounded the house. With a fresh coat of white on the ground, it was almost postcard-perfect.

On the outside, at least.

She sighed again and went inside where the signs of construction and refurbishment were all around her in the form of scaffolding against the two-story fireplace and lumber stacked in the dining room that would eventually be a state-of-the-art media room. The two-man construction crew's progress was coming along more slowly than she'd have liked, but she'd had to hire them in from Bozeman and she was lucky to get them on site for more than three days of the week.

Nevertheless, though the going was slow, she couldn't fault the quality of their work. Plus, they'd come in with the most reasonable bid.

When it was her own money on the line, she couldn't afford to call in the same companies her family usually used. Nor did she want to chance any of her vendors reporting back to them about her business here. She'd dealt with that situation far too often, too.

She worked her way around enormous paint buckets and went upstairs, heading straight for the aspirin bottle first.

Pack light, Russ had decreed. At least that was something she *did* know how to do. When he stomped through the front door a while later to find her already sitting in one of the oversize suede wing chairs that had come with the Hopping H, she allowed herself the indulgence of enjoying the surprise on his face.

Of course, he masked that surprise quickly. "The water troughs for the stock were frozen over, but I broke it up. And the horses are low on feed."

She crossed her high-heeled boots at the ankle. "Shall I run to the supermarket?" she asked sweetly. She knew she was low on feed. She was low on everything. Unfortunately, she'd *thought* she could trust Harlan, who'd assured her that he'd put in the appropriate orders long before he and his brother walked off the job.

Russ ignored her sarcasm. His gaze swept the interior of the house, undoubtedly judging the renovation mess with his usual criticism. "That thing hooked up?" He nodded toward the ancient black phone that sat on the table she'd pushed against one wall to use as a temporary desk.

"Yes."

He reached for it and didn't seem at all slowed by the old-fashioned rotary dial. For all she knew, he hadn't moved into the current century with push-button phones, either.

His phone call was brief, though, and he hung up, looking at her over her shoulder. "You'll have a delivery by early next week. In the meantime, I'll have one of my guys stock you up."

How simple he made it sound. She'd been calling the feed supply manager every day for the past week.

Being angry that he'd accomplished what she could not seem to, though, was not going to get her anywhere.

Russ had helped. That was the bottom line. And she was working hard on the whole okay-to-accept-help concept.

It did *not* come naturally to her.

"Thank you." She dashed her hands down the sleeves of her ivory leather jacket. "Will the animals be all right while we're gone?"

He looked vaguely amused. "You want pet-sitters or something?"

She felt her cheeks flush. "I want *you* to tell me what I need to know. Remember?"

"The stock'll be fine. I'll assign Joey to work over here. Why'd you take down the wall that used to be by the staircase?"

"The rooms down here are too small. Who is Joey?"

"One of my hands. He's young, but he's reliable. If you're planning to change everything inside the house here, why buy it in the first place?"

She pushed to her feet, looping the strap of her overnight bag over her shoulder. "I'm not changing everything."

He lifted his brows, looking at the evidence. "Could've fooled me. So how long's it going to take before you're ready?"

"I am ready."

He looked up the staircase. The old iron balusters and rail had been removed, leaving the treads out in the open. "Up there, I suppose."

"Excuse me?"

"Your suitcases."

She jiggled her overnighter. "You did recommend packing light, didn't you?" He'd ordered it, actually.

Like some royal decree. It would have served him right if she'd loaded up every piece of luggage she possessed.

Of course, she'd come to Montana with only a few pieces. The rest was back in Atlanta. Useless and left behind along with everything else from her life.

Her *former* life, she reminded herself.

Things were different now, because she was making them different.

"Are you going to stand here all morning critiquing my renovations or shall we get going?"

He looked her over, head to toe, and she twisted the wide leather strap harder around her hand. "*What?*"

He shook his head and grabbed the overnight case from her. "Let's get moving."

She refrained from pointing out that she hadn't been the one standing around. She followed him back out to the car that he'd once again parked in front of the house and this time didn't bother fruitlessly waiting for him to open her door.

She kept her focus out the side window as they made the drive from her house to his. It wasn't that great a distance. Less than ten miles, she figured. Yet the silent drive seemed almost interminable.

"Wait here." He finally stopped behind a modest two-story house and got out before she could even summon an argument.

He left the car running, and she crossed her arms, watching him take the back porch steps in one long stride.

She could hear the squeak of the storm door despite the distance, and then he disappeared into the house.

In comparison to the Hopping H, Russ's house

looked about a quarter of the size. The siding was painted white. The shutters around the windows both up and down were black. From what she could see, craning her head around inside her car, the roof looked sound.

Other than that, the house was decidedly plain.

She nibbled at her thumb, wondering if Russ had wanted the Hopping H's ranch house, as well as the land. Maybe that was why he'd seemed to look at her renovations with such criticism.

She sat back quickly when she saw the storm door move again, and was sliding her sunglasses onto her nose when he got back in the car after tossing his own small duffel atop her overnighter in the minuscule space behind the seats. As she'd done, he'd changed clothes, as well.

This time, his boots weren't spit-shined.

"We'll grab a charter at the airstrip and catch a commercial route outta Bozeman."

She tucked her tongue between her teeth as she mentally calculated the cost of a private charter. The McFarlanes owned more than one corporate jet, but her finances these days didn't necessarily run to such extravagances. Not when she had nearly every dime she possessed tied up in the Hopping H.

But a lifetime of pride kept her from uttering a single peep.

The airfield was located near the Thunder Canyon Resort and they left her car parked in the lot there. Melanie pulled out her credit card and passed it over before they could even bring up the subject of paying for the charter. Russ, however, gave a grimace and pulled out his wallet.

She was used to always paying the bills. With her family's wealth, it always seemed expected. Even by men. And though she had to be careful, she still felt odd about putting her card back in her purse. "Purchasing plane tickets another thing that's a husband's job?"

"Be useful," he suggested, heaping on more outrageousness. "Go find me a cup of coffee." His lips quirked up, definitely waiting for a reaction.

Standing there at the small counter while *he* took care of the finances was nothing she felt comfortable doing, so she merely arched her eyebrow at him and strolled, instead, over to one of the seats lined up below a window that overlooked the airstrip.

He didn't exactly look surprised by her failure to jump to his demand, and she ended up feeling thoroughly uncharitable when he returned with not only his own insulated cup of coffee, but a second cup for her, as well.

"It's the only kind of tea they had," he said, flipping her a paper-wrapped teabag.

"Thank you."

"Pilot'll be ready soon." He sipped the hot brew. "You probably fly private all the time."

"Not lately." She studiously dipped the teabag in the steaming water. "You?"

"When I have to." His gaze passed her for the windows overlooking the airstrip.

"Is that often?"

A muscle flexed in his hard jaw. "Not anymore."

And after that, he said no more. His silence didn't bother her, though. She had no particular desire to share her life story, either.

After that, it seemed an alarmingly short time before Melanie found herself strapped into the rear seat of the smallest plane she'd ever seen, much less been flown in. Only four seats in the horribly small cabin, with Russ in one of the front two, alongside the pilot, whom he briefly introduced as "Mac."

The middle-aged pilot with a toothpick clenched between his teeth seemed about as taciturn as Russ, and as the tiny plane took flight, she could only pray that Mac was as capable a pilot as Russ was reportedly a rancher.

But every time the small plane bumped and jolted, she had to swallow a gasp.

She didn't know how long they'd been in the air when Russ pulled off the headphones that matched the pair Mac wore and looked back at her, undoubtedly taking in her clenched hands on the armrests.

"Thought you'd be used to flying." He had to raise his voice to be heard above the plane's engine. The plane's *one* engine.

What happened if that engine failed?

"Enormous flying buses, yes." Ones with multiple engines. She uncurled her fingers that were beginning to cramp. "And when it's not a commercial flight, the McFarlane company planes are…somewhat larger than this." They were jets. Outfitted with every conceivable comfort.

The morning sunlight was slanting across his face through the plane's windows, turning his brown eyes a lighter, amber shade. "You want to live in Thunder Canyon, you'd better get used to roughing it a little."

Melanie thought she heard Mac cover up a laugh.

Her cheeks warmed. She could only imagine how

spoiled both men seemed to think she was. "I wouldn't term riding in any sort of plane as *roughing* it." She didn't need to lean forward to be heard, because the space between her row of seats and his was about the size of a postage stamp. "And this four-seater experience isn't going to scare me into running back home, if that's what you were hoping."

His lips twisted. "You've stuck it out six months already. I gave up hoping after five." He turned back around in his seat and pulled his headphones back into place.

Her imagination was really working overtime, because she could have sworn that there had been a hint of admiration in his voice.

Chapter Five

The first thing they did upon arriving in Las Vegas was ditch their coats, for the temperature was a good twenty degrees higher than it was in Montana.

They took a cab from the airport to the Marriage Bureau, and all the while Russ watched Melanie's face pale a degree with each step. Filling out the forms. When he handed over cash for the fee. When they left the building a short while later, marriage license in hand.

"How'd you get to be thirty without ever marrying?" He'd looked at the application form she'd filled out when they'd handed them over. He was relieved now to see a flash of ire show in her face at his impolitic question. Ire was better than that tense, nervous look that was so much at odds with the uppity woman he'd come to know.

"It's not a crime," she said in her snippiest back-east voice.

"Nobody ever asked you, huh?"

Her jaw dropped slightly. "It's a wonder *you're* not still married," she returned. "What woman in her right mind would possibly give up such a *sensitive* spouse?" She stepped to the curb and waved down a cab with the ease of someone who'd been doing it most of their life.

He hitched the strap of her overnighter and his duffel higher over one shoulder. Damned if his own duffel wasn't heavier. "Who says she's the one who gave me the boot? Maybe it was the other way around."

She slanted him a look as a cab slid to a stop at the curb in front of her, as obediently as a well-trained poodle. "Of course it was," she said as kindly as if she were speaking to someone mentally deficient. She pulled open the rear door and slid inside.

Russ tossed the luggage in the front seat before following her into the back. "Closest, cheapest wedding chapel," he told the driver.

Melanie huffed slightly and crossed her arms over her chest. She turned her head away, looking out the side window, and didn't speak again until the cab deposited them outside a small, white chapel with a tall steeple.

There were two couples ahead of them, both of whom couldn't seem to keep their hands off their intendeds. Which was a good thing, or Russ figured the way Melanie stood as far from him as possible at one side of the waiting area, seemingly transfixed by the wall of photographs, would have drawn some curious looks. The ceremonies ahead of them weren't exactly long affairs, and when it came time for him and Melanie, he saw the way she swallowed and seemed to pull up her shoulders in preparation.

Less like a fighter getting ready to enter the ring than a prisoner facing sentencing.

On that, he could relate.

He eyed her. She wore ivory jeans and an ivory turtleneck that clung faithfully to her curves. The only color about her was her vibrant hair. "You want flowers?"

She gave a sharp shake of her head.

The gray-haired clerk who'd been trying to up-sell their basic wedding package looked disapproving. "Here." She handed over a bouquet of pink plastic roses. "They're included."

Melanie looked reluctant.

"Go ahead, *dear,*" Russ urged. "They'll look so pretty on our complimentary photograph."

She took the small bouquet. "Thank you," she told the woman without a hint of the annoyance that was in the look she gave Russ.

"Good luck to you, honey," the clerk whispered to her, casting a skeptical eye over Russ as she took their fee and waved them toward the front of the excruciatingly cheerful chapel.

Russ couldn't tell if the man standing in front of the plastic flower-bedecked altar was a minister or not, and didn't much care. "Keep it brief," he told the man.

"In a hurry for the honeymoon," the man said easily. "Well, you came to the right place. Brief is what we specialize in here."

"Goody," he heard Melanie whisper under her breath.

"All right now. I'm Pastor Frank." He waved at the young couple standing to one side of the altar. "My son and daughter will be your witnesses. If you would join hands?"

Russ nodded at the witnesses and grabbed Melanie's hand. It was as cold as ice, but at least she didn't pull it away from him.

A few "I do's" and several snapshots from the digital camera that Pastor Frank had whipped out of his pocket, and two minutes later, they were walking back out into the sun, duly wedded.

Melanie yanked her hand away from his and slid on her sunglasses. The digital film disk they'd been given was dumped unceremoniously into the trash can outside the door.

"You hungry?"

"No." She fiddled with the plain gold band that had also been included in the price of their wedding ticket, sliding it back and forth over her knuckle. "But you probably are."

"I'm touched. Already showing wifely concern."

The ring came off her finger and was stowed inside that ivory purse of hers.

"You're gonna have to put that back on when we get back to Thunder Canyon."

"I'll wear it when I need to." Her voice was even. "Maybe cheap gold doesn't bother you, but it makes my skin itch."

The gold band on Russ's finger seemed to burn into his flesh, but it had nothing to do with the inexpensive metal. "We packed for overnight, but we could try to catch a flight back to Bozeman. Or we can still get a room and do it in the morning."

Her chin jerked a little at that.

"Get a *flight* in the morning," he clarified, swallowing a bite of laughter. "Trust me, Red. Only way you and I would be doing what you're naughty little imagination is conjuring is if you pleaded."

"In your dreams," she replied loftily.

Unfortunately, that was already a problem. Not that she needed to know that. And he sure in hell didn't intend to do anything about it. Sex with his paper-only wife would only lead to trouble. "We'll fly back in the morning, then." He took her arm as they entered a crosswalk and joined the throng of people crossing the street. "When's the last time you were in Vegas?"

She gestured vaguely toward one of the newest hotels towering over the skyline. "At the opening."

"You don't have any McFarlane hotels here."

"No." She looked out over the strip. "Not McFarlane's style."

"Wouldn't think a guest ranch in Thunder Canyon would be McFarlane's style, either."

"It will be." That determination she never seemed to turn off rang through her words. "Not all of our hotels are monoliths of traditional style and elegance, you know. The first hotel my brother, Connor, opened was in an unused railway station in Seattle. It's won awards, even."

"But I'll bet they still put a McFarlane Mint on the bed pillows with the turndown service."

She lifted her shoulder. "So? Those mints are good. We have exclusive rights to them. Have you had one?"

He and Nola had spent their wedding night in McFarlane House Boston, and she'd bought a box of the expensive things in the gift shop to bring back to Thunder Canyon. It hadn't satisfied her yen for luxury for very long, though. "A long time ago."

They could have chosen any one of the mile-long hotels looming around them to stay at. But he spotted a small diner tucked between two fenced-off construction zones and headed toward it instead, pulling her along with him.

The inside was crowded, the hum of voices and Christmas music just shy of a din. Yet there were two stools available at the counter and he made his way toward them. He dropped their suitcases on the floor between them and handed her one of the laminated menus that were tucked between a jar of mustard and a bottle of ketchup.

"I'm not very hungry."

"Eat anyway. You're too skinny."

Her lips tightened. "Women don't like hearing that any more than they want to hear that they're too heavy."

He stuck his menu back among the condiments. "You don't need me to tell you that you're beautiful. You're just even thinner now than when you first came to Thunder Canyon. You can't play at ranching if you're collapsing from hunger."

"Hey there, folks." A blond waitress deftly settled glasses of ice water in front of them. "What can I get for you today?"

"I'll have the Caesar salad," Melanie ordered, looking disconcerted.

"With chicken," Russ added.

He felt Melanie's low sigh.

"I'll take the burger special," he ordered. "And iced tea."

"Sure thing, hon." The waitress scribbled on her order pad, stuck it in on the pass-through to the kitchen, and grabbed the coffeepot for her next customer all in one smooth motion. Minutes later, it seemed, she was back, sliding their plates onto the counter and dropping their check facedown beside his plate. "Give a yell if you need anything," she said, already pivoting back toward the pass-through to pick up another order.

Melanie, he noticed, did more poking at her food than eating, while he managed to inhale half of his hamburger and fries.

He pinched the bridge of his nose and wished that he hadn't noticed. "Is there a particular hotel where you'd like to stay?"

"It'll be less expensive off the strip."

Since when would the McFarlane princess care about expense?

They were sitting at a counter in a damn-near cheap diner, yet she kept one hand resting neatly in her lap atop the paper napkin she'd spread there, and the other—the one doing all the delicate poking at the lettuce—looked as if it were holding priceless silver rather than a water-spotted fork with a bent tine. "That's not what I asked."

She shook her head. "I have no preference." She gave him a fleeting glance. "You'll just say that selecting our lodging is a husband's job."

Which made him sound like a throwback to the dark ages. Not that he hadn't earned it, given the way he'd been needling her since they came to their damn fool agreement. "You probably know people here in the business, don't you?"

"Yes." She poked at her lettuce some more. He

wasn't certain, but he thought she might be hiding the thin slices of chicken beneath it. "And if I checked into one of their hotels—with my *husband*—word would get back to my family before we can so much as blink."

"That's what you wanted, wasn't it?"

"I'd prefer to be the one to break the news to them." She looked up at him. "Do you want *your* parents to learn from someone other than you that you've gotten married?"

"My parents are deceased."

Her brows drew together in a quick frown. "I'm sorry. Do you have other family?"

She meant brothers and sisters, undoubtedly. And he didn't.

The only family he had was Ryan.

"No," he said flatly.

The edge of her teeth sank into her perfectly formed lower lip at his flat answer. "Okay, but surely you can still appreciate the situation."

He flagged down their waitress. "Is there a phone book I can use?"

"What're you looking for?"

"Hotels."

She reached under the counter and pulled out a local guide. "That's all you'll need. More tea?"

He shook his head, and slid the glossy booklet toward Melanie. "Pick a place where you *don't* know the management, then."

She set down her fork, dotted her mouth delicately with the corner of her napkin and reached for the brochure. She flipped through it for a moment. "There." She tapped one page.

"That's a non-gaming hotel."

"Do you have a gambling problem?"

He gave her a look.

She smiled faintly and looked again at the brochure. "This one, then."

He glanced at it. Truth was, he didn't much care where they stayed. "Give me your cell phone. I'll call in for a room."

"Rooms."

He lifted his eyebrow. "But, babe. It's our wedding night."

The look she gave him in return was so arid he felt the need to drink down the dregs of his iced tea. "Rooms, then," he allowed. It was just as well. Sharing a room—even one with two beds and plenty of space between them—was probably not the wisest of courses.

"Good. But I'm sorry. I don't have my cell phone."

"Forget it back in Thunder Canyon?"

She looked vaguely chagrinned. "I…yes."

There'd been a pay phone on the outside of the diner. "Finish eating. I'll go make sure they've got rooms with an *S*." He took the check with him. Might as well pay the girl at the counter by the door while he was at it.

Melanie's shoulders sagged the moment Russ moved away from the counter and headed out of the busy diner. She could only pray that she relaxed a little over the next several months. Because if she maintained this level of tension, she'd probably have a heart attack before her arrangement with Russ ended.

"You two been married long?" The blond waitress was back, topping off Melanie's water.

"Less than an hour now."

"Ah." Smiling, the woman leaned her hip against the counter. "Vegas wedding." She waved her hand, showing off her wedding band. "Worked for me and my Jed. Twenty-seven years now. Back then he was a handsome cuss like your man. I had to make sure all the other ladies knew he was taken. Bet you do, too."

Melanie managed a smile. "Twenty-seven years is a long time in this day and age. Congratulations."

"Not so long, really, when you've got love between you." The waitress winked. "And plenty of lovin', if you know what I mean."

Melanie could feel her cheeks flush.

The propensity for blushing was definitely one of the downsides of being a redhead by nature. She'd dyed her hair brown once, back when she was in college, but that hadn't done a single thing toward alleviating that particular nuisance.

"Okay." Russ returned. "We're set. Did you eat *any* of that chicken?"

"She's a bride," the waitress defended cheerfully. "She's got more things on her mind. I can box it all up for you, though, if you'd like."

Melanie shook her head. "That's kind, but no, thank you."

The waitress clearly didn't take offense. She just smiled. "I hope y'all have a long, happy life together."

"Thank you." Melanie switched the strap of her purse from her bent knee to her shoulder and rose. She was painfully aware of the hand that Russ put on the small of her back as she preceded him from the diner.

"Guess you didn't mind *her* knowing we got hitched."

The sun was on a downward slide into late afternoon. "I don't mind my family knowing we have married." That had been her plan, after all, in order to hide the fact that she was in over her head where the ranch was concerned. "I do, however, care about the method in which they are informed. How are you planning to tell your friends back in Thunder Canyon?"

"Red, by the time we get back there, Mac will have done half the work. He'll call his wife and tell her that we were on our way to Vegas and the game of telephone tag will have begun. Once the gossip makes it back to Grant or Steph—who know we spent the night together— they'll be speculating plenty. Oh, jeez. You're all pale again. If you'd just have eaten some chicken, maybe I wouldn't have to worry about you passing out on me."

"I am *not* going to pass out on you." And she didn't need any chicken to eat when she was feeling as if she were already the biggest chicken on the planet. "Do we need a cab, or can we walk from here?"

He stepped to the curb and let out a piercing whistle.

A cab veered out of traffic and stopped next to them.

"Impressive," Melanie murmured after he'd given the driver the name of the hotel. "Did you learn *that* ability in Thunder Canyon?"

"Boston." He grimaced. "I lived there for about three of the longest months of my life."

For the first time all day, Melanie felt some speck of humor. "Not much of a city boy?" She didn't have to wait for his answer to know that he wasn't.

If there was one thing that she could say about Russ Chilton, it was that *rural* pretty much flowed from his pores. He didn't look like a man who could be contained within the busy congestion of a city. Instead, he looked like a man who could stand in the center of vast, open spaces and wrangle every acre to his will.

"Not much," he agreed. "I was born and raised in Thunder Canyon and that's where they'll bury me."

"Despite the growth that's been occurring there?" She knew he hadn't just picked her personally to disapprove of because she'd bought out the Hopping H. He'd disapproved of her plan to buy Grant Clifton's property, too. In fact, he'd been a vocal opponent of many developments around the thriving town.

"I'm a rancher, babe. Ain't no way I'm going to love having the town start to encroach around my space. But you don't just stop loving something 'cause it has the nerve to change on you. Thunder Canyon's in my cells and neither one of us is going anywhere."

She smiled slightly. "Thank you."

His brows quirked. "For what?"

"Proving that I did choose the right person to help me."

He grimaced, looking annoyed. As if he'd given away the secret to some family recipe. "Then you'd better get over it," he said. "Because *I'm* only helping you to get my hands on your land."

"It's a refreshing change, at least." The cabbie came to a stop in front of the hotel she'd selected in the brochure.

"Change from what?" He passed over enough cash to cover the modest fare.

"The men who only wanted to get their hands on my money."

He snorted and reached past her to push open the door. "Must not be much in the way of men," he said. "Or they'd be wanting to get their hands on *you*."

Chapter Six

Russ's assessment was still ringing in Melanie's ears when they checked out of the hotel the next morning and made their way back to Montana and Thunder Canyon.

It was ironic, really. Because, true to his word, Russ had arranged two rooms. Adjoining rooms—but that didn't mean they'd allowed that closed door to ever become a passageway between them.

Which meant that she'd probably misinterpreted the meaning behind his words altogether.

He didn't want to get his hands on her. The only thing she represented to him was a path to the Hopping H.

Aside from taking in a late dinner show with a local comedian—they had to do *something* to pass the evening, he'd reasoned—Russ and she hadn't spent more than five minutes in one another's company.

Not that she cared.

Heavens no.

Unless it had something to do with the ranch, the less time they spent together the better. She knew there were areas where she lacked experience. Being around him any more than necessary just seemed to underscore that particular fact.

It was late in the afternoon when they finally picked up her car from the lot at the airstrip and drove back to the Hopping H. She wasn't overly surprised when, once again, he dropped her at the house before driving out to the barns.

She carried her overnight bag inside and unpacked it upstairs in the bedroom that she'd selected for her own use because it had an eastern exposure and she liked waking with the sun. The only thing it lacked was an attached bathroom, but that particular luxury was going to have to wait.

She had the accommodations for the guest rooms to worry about first.

Feeling about as nervous as a cat, she wandered back downstairs.

She and Russ were married. *Now what?*

She prowled the kitchen where, fortunately, the renovations had already been completed, and set a fresh pot of tea brewing. After the warmth of Nevada, she felt chilled to the bone.

Or maybe that was just her nerves.

The message light on her answering machine was blinking. Leaving the tea to steep, she sat down at her makeshift desk and hit the button. She had half a page of notes by the time she heard water running from the kitchen. Russ must have come in through the back door.

She repeated one of the messages from the warehouse providing the mattresses she'd chosen for the guest rooms to get the phone number right. Unfortunately, the mattresses were on back order and it didn't look as if they'd be available before February.

She'd hoped to be open for business in February.

Sighing, she erased the message and the last one began.

"Melanie," her father's deep voice rang out of the machine, nearly startling her right off the wooden crate she was using as a chair. "Call me *now.*"

That was all.

She looked at the time the message had come in and her stomach sank down to her toes.

Four o'clock yesterday.

About the time that she and Russ had gone to their separate rooms.

"He didn't sound happy." Russ came into the room, running a dish towel over his damp forearms that he'd obviously just washed. "Who was it?"

"My father."

"Does he always sound like he's got a stick up his—"

"Pretty much," she cut him off. "Where I'm concerned, at least." She deliberately turned away from the telephone, the notes from the messages about her renovations *and* her father's demand. "So, where do we start?"

His brown gaze flicked from her face to the ancient telephone. "Why where *you* are concerned?"

"It doesn't matter." She yanked out a banker's box

crammed with records from beneath the table. "I've tried to make as much order out of all this as I could. They seem to be the only ranch-related records left by the previous owner." Might as well jump in with both feet. He'd learn soon enough what a deplorable state the ranch records were in.

He looked as if he wanted to pursue the matter about her father, which she knew was unlikely. He only cared about his cut of the Hopping H and that was just fine with her.

He looked in the box. Pulled out one of the file folders and flipped through it. "I guess it could be worse. These records are over a year old, though. Anything more recent?"

"Harlan was supposed to be keeping up with things, but I didn't find anything in the office except this stuff. No inventory of the stock, no invoices for supplies or anything."

He looked grim. "What about the work that's going on inside here and inside the bunkhouse?"

"Not that the renovations should matter to you, but that's all here." She pulled another filing unit—this one on wheels with two drawers—out for him to see. There was no way he could find fault with her organization there. And there was also no way that she would allow him to think he had a right to judge her work on that score.

"Everything about the H matters to me, until our deal is done and the land is split. Maybe I want to make sure you're not planning to turn this place into some pink palace or something."

She made a face. "Please. Give me some credit, will you?" She pulled out a portfolio and flipped it open atop the table to reveal the architectural renderings she'd commissioned. "As you can see, when it's finished, the bunkhouse can be rented out either as a single or double unit. Very highly priced units, which I know I'll be able to command, considering the view and access the place has to the mountains. It'll be ski in and ski out, even. That's a big selling factor."

She slid the oversize drawing aside to reveal several more, feeling the same surge of excitement that she'd experienced when she and the architect had worked out the design plans. "The house here, of course, will be the main lodge. The exterior won't change much. It's already wonderfully rustic with the stone and rough-hewn logs. Mostly it'll be landscape work around the lodge, but obviously that has to wait until spring."

"What kind of landscaping?"

"A formal English garden, of course." She waited a beat. "Adding a few retaining walls. Wildflowers. Nothing that will look out of place here, I assure you. Now, inside, the current layout *will* change. We'll have six guest bedrooms with several common areas." She nodded her head toward the former dining room. "A media room that'll keep even the most demanding guest entertained. By summer, I also want to be ready to break ground on four cabins down by the creek. They'll allow some privacy for families, but also be somewhat more affordable than the bunkhouse would be." She dragged out the last sheets. "Riding arena, heated outdoor pool, sauna, workout room. We'll serve family-style meals here in the lodge. You probably noticed the improvements already done in the kitchen. For fine dining, shopping and such, guests can head over to the resort. I also hope to make a deal with Grant for golf packages once the course is finished over there. We'll be considerably smaller than the Thunder Canyon Resort, naturally, and I'll be playing on that very fact to appeal to guests who want a more intimate setting."

He took the corner of one of the heavy sheets and pulled it closer, studying the overall map of the entire property. "Your fishing dock should be here." He jabbed a spot on the creek farther north of where she'd located it in relative proximity to the cabins.

"That's too far away. If the dock is here where I've planned, parents will be able to watch their children from their front porches."

"Your call, but they won't catch a lick. Fish don't bite down there. They *do,* here." He tapped the map. "Anything south of that bend they'll just be wasting bait."

"How do you know?"

His gaze lifted to hers and she had to suck in a hard breath at the lazy twinkle there. "Told you, darlin'. I've been fishing that creek since I was knee-high to a grasshopper. Now, if you don't care about your guests being able to actually *land* a fish, then it doesn't matter."

She pulled the sheet closer to her, staring at it. Would it be possible to move the location of the cabins? She'd have to consult her architect. "But I do want them to catch fish. I want them to ski and to hike and horseback ride and taste what life is like on a real ranch. I want them to be able to do anything and everything that this corner of the world offers up with such glory."

His silence was deafening and she looked up at him, grimacing a little. The twinkle was gone from his eyes, replaced by something she couldn't quite identify. Something that made her feel distinctly...edgy.

She began gathering up the pages, sliding them back into the protective sleeve of the portfolio. "Sorry. I tend to get carried away thinking about all this."

His hand dropped over hers, stilling her movement. "I would hope so, considering the lengths you're willing to go to in order to make it happen. I may not think they're the greatest of plans, but that doesn't mean I don't respect the fact that you're giving something that matters to you your best shot."

His fingers were warm. Long. Calloused and blunt-tipped, with nails cut unceremoniously short.

And heaven help her, but she felt ridiculously breathless. "Well." She stopped and cleared her throat of the frog that seemed lodged there and continued shuffling together the sheets. His hand fell away. "Thanks for that."

He bunched the dish towel between his hands. "What're you going to tell your dad when you call him?"

Her shoulders tightened up again. "It's too coincidental to think that he called when he did just to chat. First of all, Donovan McFarlane doesn't *chat* with anyone, least of all me." She slid the portfolio back into the space between the table legs and the wall where it wouldn't be disturbed. "He already knows we, um, eloped."

"How? You might have a recognizable name, but we weren't exactly being trailed around by paparazzi down there."

She brushed her fingertips through her hair, restlessly moving away from the desk. "My father tends to keep track of me," she said with massive understatement. Though she'd thought he would have given up the practice once she'd left her position in Atlanta.

Why follow her, double-checking her every move, when she was no longer running a McFarlane property? It wasn't as if her personal life held any interest to her family.

The only thing the McFarlanes concerned themselves with was business. Period.

In that, she was very *much* a McFarlane. Whether or not her family trusted her business acumen, she knew it was the one thing she was good at.

When it came to personal relationships, though? She was completely out of her depth.

She picked up her leather jacket where she'd dropped it over a sawhorse and shook it out.

Russ was watching her, skepticism written all over his carved features. "Keeps track of you how?"

"It doesn't matter. It has nothing to do with us."

"It does if he's supposed to be thinking you and I are married. How's that going to look to him if he sees that you're living over here and I'm at the Flying J?"

She jammed her coat over one of the wooden hooks by the front door. "I just…well, I didn't get that far in my thinking, all right?"

His eyebrows shot up. "You can come up with a plan like that—" he waved his arm toward the portfolio "—for the Hopping H, but not work out details like this?" He shoved his hand through his hair.

"I didn't think he'd still be interested in examining every decision I make! I knew I'd be seeing them over

Christmas—heaven forbid that I shouldn't be present for the family's command-performance party—and when they gave me the third degree over why I hadn't caved in and returned to the fold, I would tell them that I was too busy with my brand-new marriage and the guest ranch."

"So all this is just a way of avoiding going back to work for the McFarlane empire?"

She let out a shaking breath. "No. Of course not."

He shook his head. "I don't have a clue how any of that makes sense, but it ain't *my* family."

Only now, because of the marriage license they'd both signed, that wasn't strictly accurate anymore.

Melanie felt no inclination, however, toward pointing out that detail to him. He was probably already well aware of it, anyway. "There are still rooms upstairs that we haven't begun reno on. If you wouldn't mind spending a, um, a night or two here—just enough to pass on appearance's sake—I'm sure we can make you comfortable."

"Is that a royal *we?*"

"Excuse me?"

"Who else here is going to ensure my comfort, other than *you?* You don't have any other staff."

"Yet." She folded her hands together in front of her waist. "Habit, I'm afraid. I've been working in one of our hotels since I was a teenager. Everything is always the collective. We. Us."

"This isn't a hotel, *yet*—" he returned pointedly "—and the only collective around here is you, and me."

A disturbingly inappropriate image of the two of

them being "collective" leaped into her mind and stuck there. "Shall I prepare a room for you, or not?"

He let out a breath. "Might as well. There's a boat-load of work to be done over here and spending time running back and forth between my place and here is just silly."

Her stomach sank. "What work?"

"The roof on the barn is leaking. You've got fence that is down all over the place, which is probably why the quick count I made of the cattle is down. Two mares look to be in foal, and if you want to have horses safe enough for your guests to be riding, we've got work to do, because I'll bet my boots that half of 'em are already barn sour."

"I don't even know what that's supposed to mean. But how can I have two horses in foal?"

He lifted his eyebrows. "Do you need me to draw a diagram?"

Her face turned hot. "I meant that I don't have any stallions." She wasn't so unknowledgeable that she didn't know that particular point.

"Gestation for a horse is about 340 days. They were obviously covered before you bought the H." The corner of his lips kicked up. "And by that, I mean they were—"

"I know what it means," she snapped.

"There's probably record of it somewhere."

She felt thoroughly judged and left wanting. "I told you, I've unearthed every record about this place that I could find."

He shrugged. "Too bad. If you could determine the sire, they'd be worth more. But you can still consider it a couple of bonuses. You're increasing the number of head without paying stud fees."

"How long do you think before they'll foal?"

"At a guess? Another few months."

"Do you, um, have any experience with that sort of thing?" Horses in foal meant more veterinarian bills than she'd budgeted for, too. Unless Russ's experience also ran to horse breeding.

"Some."

She moistened her lips. She had more immediate things to worry about than equine labor and delivery. "Is this barn-sour thing going to end up costing me money?"

He gave her a calculating look. "Barn sour just means the horses are getting lazy—they don't want to leave the barn. Will be a problem when you're wanting to send out your high-paying guests on leisurely twilight horseback rides."

"So what do I do about that?"

"They'll need exercising to get over it. Regular exercise. So add riding lessons to everything else you need to learn."

Hallelujah. Something she could manage herself. "I know how to ride."

His eyebrows lifted. "You don't say."

"Eastern," she admitted.

He didn't quite look scornful. "It's better than nothing, at least. When's the last time you rode?"

She wished he hadn't asked. "A few years ago."

His lashes narrowed, pinning her with a don't-mess-with-me look. "How few?"

She sighed. "About ten. But it's like riding a bicycle, isn't it? One never really forgets."

"You can tell that to your fanny tomorrow after you've spent a few hours in the saddle. Here." He tossed her the damp dish towel. "Make up the room. I'll be back later."

She'd managed—albeit poorly—on her own for the past week, yet the nervous jolt that ran through her as he headed for the door was distinctly alarming. It wasn't as if Harlan and Danny had stayed in the house with her. They'd lived in the bunkhouse.

She squeezed the towel between her fists. "Where are you going?"

"Missing me already? Ain't that sweet." He flipped out the pockets of his shearling coat. "I don't carry underwear in my pockets."

She would *not* blush. "Very funny."

A smile was playing around his lips. He turned up his coat collar and pulled open the heavy, oversize front door. "I've gotta take care of some things at my own place."

Of course he did. She was being a ninny. She *preferred* that he spend only as much time as it took for her to learn what she could from him.

"I'll be back before nightfall. And if I'm not," he shot her a twisted grin, "keep the bed warm."

She flushed. "You'd better bring your own electric blanket, then, because that's the only thing that's going to keep it warm for you around here."

His teeth flashed and he shut the door behind him.

Melanie exhaled, only to nearly jump out of her skin when the old phone let out a shrill ring.

She crossed the room toward the telephone. There was no such convenience as caller ID on the old model, but she didn't have to make a wild guess as to who would be on the other line. And when she answered, her guess was confirmed.

"What kind of mess have you gotten into now, Melanie? I suppose your mother or I will have to come and clean things up for you there."

Her jaw suddenly ached, as if she'd been clenching her teeth for a lifetime. "Hello, Donovan. How nice to hear from you."

"Well? What do you have to say for yourself? Your mother is in quite a state. Obviously this man you've gone off and married yourself to is someone entirely unsuitable, or you'd have told us about him yourself. Instead, I hear it through the grapevine!"

A darned effective grapevine, she acknowledged, too late. They should have just flown back after their quickie wedding, because it had to have been the hotel in Vegas where that vine had obviously flourished. And she'd thought it would be safe. "Russ is not unsuitable." She pushed her fingers against the pain between her eyes.

"He drags you off to Las Vegas for some cheap wedding? I suppose I can find a judge out there to handle the annulment."

Her shoulders tightened. "Dad, I am thirty years old. I wasn't *dragged* anywhere. And there will be no annulment." Not until their six-month agreement was up, in any case, and at that point, she would be doing the arranging.

Not her controlling father.

"Good God," he sounded shocked. "Are you *pregnant?* Is that what this is all about?"

Melanie winced. Pregnant? Somehow, she doubted she was a candidate for immaculate conception. And that's what it would take, given her deplorable and absolute lack of experience in such matters. "No, I am not pregnant," she said stiffly. "But even if I were, it would be my responsibility to handle it. I'm an adult. Isn't it long past time for you to recognize that?"

"Is that what this Montana folly of yours is, then? An attempt to prove how competent you are?"

"I know I'm competent," she returned, holding on to her temper with an effort. She wasn't redheaded for nothing. "The problem is that none of *you* seem to recognize it."

"As usual, you're overreacting."

Her hand tightened on the phone. "Was it overreacting when I discovered that you'd been second-guessing every management decision I've ever made? Was it overreacting to learn that—when I'd *thought* I was in charge at McFarlane House Atlanta, as my title of general manager suggested—I was merely a figurehead? How would you like to learn that your entire staff was laughing behind your back every time you issued managerial decisions?"

"Obviously, you're hysterical. Of course we monitored you in Atlanta."

Her eyes blurred with hot, unwanted tears. They'd already had this argument, nearly a year ago, when she'd discovered what a laughingstock her own parents had made of her. Donovan and Charise McFarlane just did *not* get it. They implicitly trusted every decision that her brother made, but when it came to her?

She cleared her throat. "Thank you for calling with your best wishes, Father. I'll be sure to extend them to my husband."

"Melanie—"

She set the phone down, cutting off his annoyed voice.

Then she slid down onto the floor and pressed her face against her knees.

Success. That was the only thing they cared about. And the only way they'd ever believe Melanie could be successful was if she proved it. On her own.

The Hopping H *had* to succeed.

It just had to.

Chapter Seven

Russ wasn't particularly surprised when the first visitor he and Melanie had the next morning was Grant.

His old buddy found them in the horse barn where Russ was taking perhaps a little too much pleasure in watching Melanie shovel out horse manure.

She looked shocked to see Grant, and maybe a little embarrassed, too, as she dashed her hand over her tousled hair and down her grimy designer blue jeans.

The truth was, Grant—standing there in his charcoal wool coat and priccy boots—was far more her type than Russ, in his checked flannel and discount-store jeans, was, and the realization was enough to give Russ pause.

Melanie *had* been dealing with Grant often enough in the past until he'd changed his mind about selling

Clifton's Pride to her. Just because Grant was crazy in love with Steph didn't mean that Melanie couldn't have been interested in *him*.

"Let me wash up," she was saying quickly. "Get you some coffee. There's still some left from the pot in the tack room that Russ made. It's still hot."

Grant waved away the offer. "I just came to track down Russ, here."

"Of course." Melanie's brown eyes skipped over Russ. She set the handle of her pitchfork against the stall rail and moved past Russ out of the stall. "I'll leave you to it."

But Russ could already figure what Grant was there about, and he dropped his arm over Melanie's shoulders, stopping her escape. "No need for that, honey," he drawled, holding her against his side despite the resistance he could feel in her body. He'd called her skinny, and it was true, but the woman *did* possess the requisite number of curves beneath the thick blue sweatshirt she wore, and they were guaranteed to catch his unwilling interest. "Grant's probably here to offer his congratulations."

She slid her arm around his waist in a loving gesture that masked the hard little pinch she gave him.

He jerked and covered the punishing fingers with his other hand.

"So it's true, then?" Grant's sharp gaze took in them both. "You went off to Las Vegas together?"

"I told you that Mac would spread the word."

Melanie gave him a tight smile. "So you did." Her cheeks were pink, but she didn't exactly embody the whole "blushing bride" thing, and he didn't kid himself that Grant wouldn't notice that fact.

"We didn't go for the casinos," he told Grant. "We got married there."

Grant's eyes narrowed. "No kidding."

Russ held up his hand with the wedding band still in place. "No kidding."

Melanie gave a little laugh when Grant shifted his gaze to *her* bare hand. "I'd, um, be wearing mine, too, but I didn't want to lose it in, well, you know." She waved her hand at the wheel barrel she was filling with horse droppings. "Now, if you both don't mind, I'll just excuse myself for a few minutes." She ducked out from beneath Russ's arm. "I really did enjoy your party the other evening. Tell Steph again for me, if you would?" She practically skipped out of the barn, so great was her rush.

"Well?" Grant eyed him when she was gone. "What the hell are you up to?"

"Don't know what you mean."

"Right. You spend one night at the resort with the woman that you've spent the past half year bitching about and now you're *married* to her?"

"That's right."

Grant looked bewildered. "But why? Hell, man. I get that you think she's hot. But you've slept with plenty of other women without rushing off to the altar."

Russ's smile was filled with irony. If only Grant knew. Melanie was the one woman he *hadn't* slept with. Though he'd managed to imagine plenty about doing just that the night before in the too-short bed a few doors down from her bedroom, when he'd have been better off sleeping. "Better not let Steph hear you talk like that or she's gonna think you're not that hot on the idea of getting hitched yourself."

"Steph knows how I feel about her."

And Russ knew it had taken Grant long enough to admit it. "Speaking of which, the wedding still on for Christmas Day?" He grabbed the pitchfork and began quickly finishing off the work that Melanie had been laboring through.

"Yeah. But you're not going to distract me that easily. You're up to something."

"Maybe everyone else's weddings made me realize what I was missing out on."

"You've already had a wedding, and for ten years you've sworn you'd never go through one again."

"Times change." Russ's voice was pointed. "How many times lately have you reminded me of that? Now, are you going to congratulate me or not?"

"Congratulations," Grant offered skeptically. "You know, Steph's going to want to give you a party or something."

"Talk her out of it."

"Does anyone talk Steph out of anything?"

Russ grimaced wryly. "Good point."

"Does all this have something to do with Melanie buying the H?"

Russ jammed the pitchfork into the wheelbarrow and rolled it to the next stall. They'd already moved the horses outside to the riding arena. "What if it does?"

Grant sighed faintly. "She's not all bad, Russ. And you're not the kind to deliberately hurt—"

"Damn!" Annoyed, Russ tossed the pitchfork down again. He eyed his friend. "How low do you think I'd go? I didn't twist her arm. She's a big girl. She knows what she's doing. *I* know what I'm doing. So let it be."

Still, Grant looked concerned. "This doesn't have anything to do with Nola, does it?"

Russ exhaled roughly. "Hell."

"Well, she *looks* like her," Grant defended. "And I know that isn't my imagination."

"There's a damn big difference between Nola and Melanie and it goes a helluva long way past their red hair," Russ said flatly. "I'm not about to make the same mistakes this time around."

"I hope not. I remember the state you were in. I don't want to see that happen again."

He remembered the state he'd been in, too. It was a hell that he'd never quite climbed out of; just one that he'd become numb to. "That wasn't about Nola. It's about Ryan, and you damn well know it." He looked past Grant to see Melanie again. She'd pulled on a black pea coat and her hair was once again a sleek cap around her head. She'd even tossed a vivid-red knitted scarf around her neck.

How could someone with manure up to the knees on her skinny jeans manage to look so damn good?

He caught Grant watching him watching *her* and wanted to swear.

She was carrying two mugs in her hand, and she handed one to Grant, then to Russ, when she reached them. "I figured you might as well have something warm in your hands." She started to leave the barn again.

"Wait." Russ caught her hand and he realized she hadn't just combed her hair. She'd put on her wedding ring. "Grant says that Steph will want to throw a party for us."

Melanie's lips rounded. "Oh. How nice. But this is such a busy time of year, nobody should feel compelled—"

"Nonsense," Grant dismissed her reluctance. "It'll be our pleasure. Some time in the next week or two? Steph'll want to call and get down to details with you directly, I'm sure. And don't say it's not necessary. Russ has a lot of friends in this town. Everyone'll want to celebrate the good news."

"Then we can't very well refuse that, can we?" Melanie smiled graciously. "Thank you."

That gracious smile, however, didn't last once Grant had excused himself again.

She turned on Russ. "You *could* have talked him out of it."

"Why should I?"

Her hands flapped. "Well, because! You can't expect me to believe that you're comfortable with misleading all of your friends about this being some...some romantic adventure."

"I'll worry about my friends. You worry about your family."

"It's not that easy, and you know it. And who is Ryan?"

He thought about not answering, but decided against it. There were some things that they should reasonably know about one another—as long as they could keep from getting into the gritty details.

As far as he was concerned, that wouldn't be reasonable at all.

"My son." He took the pitchfork and pushed it into her hands. "Hurry up and get the rest of these stalls mucked out. Morning's wasting and we've still got to get started on exercising those nags of yours."

Melanie stared after Russ as he stomped out of the barn before she managed to find a voice through her stunned surprise.

Russ had a *son?* He was a father? A parent?

She suddenly felt as if she were looking at a photograph that had shifted dizzyingly right before her eyes.

She jogged after him, completely ignoring the three remaining stalls, and caught up to him in the tack room as he swung a saddle over his shoulder. "Wait a minute!"

"If you're not gonna shovel horsecrap, then here." He shoved a bridle and horse blanket into her arms. "At least make yourself useful." He left the tack room and unlatched the gate to the riding arena and stepped through.

"You can't just stop there, Russ. For heaven's sake. A son?"

"He's not up for discussion. That ought to be something you understand." The gate rattled back into place, hard, when he gave it a shove.

She bent down and slipped through the rails, following him. "Excuse me?" The ground was muddy and slick and her boots nearly slid out from beneath her, but she kept the tack from falling out of her hands. "I'd hardly compare my reluctance to chat about my family in the same vein as you never mentioning a *child!* Where is he? How old is he? Will you be seeing him for Christmas?"

"Boston. Ten. No."

She winced when he gave a sharp whistle that had three horses trotting obediently toward him. He deftly singled out a big bay and slid a halter over him, which he secured to a fence post. "Put the blanket over him," he ordered, brushing his palm over the horse's back. "You want to make sure there are no burrs or anything. And keep the horse's hair lying flat." Evidently satisfied, he patted the horse. "Put it here."

She tossed the red-and-black checked blanket where he said and again had to catch herself from falling right on her tush. Not that it would make much difference. She was already filthy. Her manicure was shot, and she wasn't certain she'd ever get the aroma of horse droppings out of her nostrils. "Why not?"

"Because it irritates the horse."

She grimaced. "That's not what I meant."

"I know." But he still didn't elaborate. He lifted the saddle onto the blanket, seeming to settle it as if it were air. Then he began cinching it into place with such speed she knew she couldn't have repeated the steps for herself if she'd tried. "Get the bridle on," he told her, when he'd buckled the last strap—the breast collar, he told her—in place.

"I don't know how."

"Figures," he muttered.

"Then show me!" She shook the bridle and the bit jingled. "That's what this is all about, isn't it?"

"Yeah. Let's not forget it." His fingers felt warm against her cold ones as he took the bridle. "Be quiet and watch."

She bristled. Her futile conversation with her father the night before was still too fresh in her thoughts, and she was thoroughly tired of people thinking they could order her around. "I'm not going to be quiet if I have questions."

"Fine. Ask all the questions you want, as long as they're all about tacking up this horse."

She made a face at his back. Childish, perhaps, but she still felt better. That is, until he patiently instructed her through the process—he even had her do it twice—of bridling the horse. Then he went back into the tack room for more equipment, leaving her to repeat the process on her own one last time.

He didn't check every single step when he returned, either. Just ran his fingers through Domino's forelock, straightening the black strands.

Then she just felt childish.

He was right. What business was it of hers if he didn't want to talk about his son? Obviously there was something amiss in the relationship, or he wouldn't be so reticent.

Was he a reluctant father? A stern father?

Somehow, she couldn't picture him as a total pushover.

She simply couldn't get the curiosity out of her head.

Not when he climbed up on the saddled horse— telling her he wanted to see what sort of seat all the horses were before she got in the saddle—and rode the horse in circles, several times, first around the arena, then outside of it, down past the barns, all the way over to the house and back again. Nor when he unsaddled Domino, and showed her how to groom the horse while he saddled up another and repeated the riding test.

They went through six horses in that manner, and Melanie's hands were stiff with cold, her boots freshly caked with mud, by the time he called a halt.

"Hope you have more than rabbit food for lunch inside that big ol' commercial refrigerator of yours." He carried the bucket of curry combs and brushes that he'd given her to use back into the tack room.

"I don't usually eat lunch." She tried scraping the soles of her boots on the edge of the brick path leading from the arena to the tack room, but the mud was stubbornly thick. The things would never be the same again.

"There's your first mistake. Today is a snap compared to some," he warned. "Shoveling and currying horses doesn't have squat against a day of branding and castrating."

She paled a little, her mind shying away from the images.

He obviously took no notice of her sensitivities, though. "You want to learn about being your own ranch hand, you're also gonna have to learn how to eat like one. It's hard work, princess, and keeping up the pace means keeping your body fueled." He propped his hands on his hips. The down vest he wore over a blue flannel shirt was unbuttoned, his head was bare, and he didn't seem to feel a need for gloves on his hands despite the icy nip in the air.

She, on the other hand, felt as if she would never get warm. And it wasn't even officially winter yet. "I imagine I can throw something together," she lied blithely. "I haven't starved myself yet." Though her efforts since she'd left management of McFarlane House Atlanta had been pretty basic. She was used to having an entire kitchen staff at hand. Even if she'd wanted something in the middle of the night, all she'd had to do was call down to room service, and her every taste would be satisfied.

The advantage of living in a penthouse suite in one of the finest hotels in the city.

Now, she'd become used to slathering peanut butter on top of saltine crackers and opening cans of soup to heat in the microwave. Somehow, she doubted that Russ would be satisfied with such meager offerings.

"Well?" He was clearly waiting for her to do something other than stand there like a bump on a log.

"Give me a half hour or so." She turned on her heel and strode across the brick walkway, then slid her way along the gravel the rest of the way back to the house.

Refusing to enter it wearing her filthy boots—the only maid service to clean up the floors was named Melanie McFarlane, after all—she sat down on the back steps outside the kitchen and worked them off, grimacing as her hands ended up covered in mud…and Lord knew what else…which she ended up wiping down the thighs of her jeans.

In her stocking feet, she finally went inside. She left her coat and scarf draped over the doorknob and groaned at her reflection in the powder-room mirror. Knowing that Russ hadn't been hard on her heels following her back to the house, she shimmied out of her filthy jeans, and whipped off her sweatshirt, as well, bundling them both into a ball that she dropped on top of the intimidating washing machine that stood nearly as high as she in the laundry room in the basement below the kitchen.

Then, still shivering despite the pink thermal underwear that covered her from neck to toe, she darted back up the stairs into the kitchen again. She *had* learned how to use the microwave, at least.

She'd toss something in it, then run up to her room, pull on more clean clothes that would also probably end up able to stand up on their own if her morning's experience was anything to go by, and when she was dressed again, lunch should be dinging on the microwave's timer.

She stopped at the commercial-sized freezer and pulled open one of the doors, peering inside. It was half-filled with freezer-wrapped packages, but what was inside those white block-sized chunks was anyone's guess. She'd merely transferred them from the house's original freezer to this one since she was told that running a filled freezer was more economical than running a nearly empty one.

One of these days, she supposed she should unwrap a few just to see what sort of meat was inside and figure out some method of preparing it.

She could practically hear the laughter inside her head at the notion of *her* preparing any sort of real meal. She shut it off and reached for two of the frozen dinners she'd bought for herself.

Fried chicken and vegetarian rice bowl in hand, she closed the door.

Russ was standing there, leaning back against the granite countertop. The corners of his lips were curved up, and his dark eyes were full of the devil. "Is the way you're dressed going to be part of the reason for those exorbitant fees you plan to charge?"

She flushed. Knowing that she was perfectly well covered was fine in theory. But the reality of standing there in her long underwear was another matter entirely.

So she took the offensive. "What a novel idea." The

boxes landed on the counter with a solid, frozen thud. She tugged the hem of the clinging undershirt down more firmly around her hips and spun in a slow, model-posed circle. "Maybe I'd be able to charge even more than I'd planned."

The amusement on his face didn't disappear, but it did shift in his eyes, which were studying her intently. "You might as well be naked."

It was a good thing she'd acquired some bravado in the past few months because that's what it took for her to arch her eyebrow and glance down at herself. "You think?"

He was right, of course. Every inch of her was faithfully outlined in soft pink waffle-weave. Including her tight nipples.

"Do you *ever* wear panties, or do you just prefer to carry them in your pockets?"

She managed not to choke as she tore one of the boxes right in half. So what if she didn't have on underwear beneath her underwear? To her, that seemed quite redundant. "You *could* take the high road and pretend that incident never occurred."

"I could." He pushed away from the counter and ran his finger down her back. "But what would be the fun in that?"

She nearly jumped out of her skin. "We're not here to have fun."

He gave a bark of laughter. "Spoken like a true wife." He picked up the fried chicken platter she'd revealed. "I'll take this one."

She snatched it out of his hand, shoved it in the microwave and raced up to her room and its closet full of clothes, his laughter following her.

What disturbed her more, however, was the way every ridge of her spine still tingled from his touch.

She'd never before been distracted by a man, but she was very much afraid that this time, where Russ was concerned, there was nothing *but* distraction.

Chapter Eight

After just two weeks of tutelage from Russ, Melanie knew that she'd never worked so hard in her entire life. Which wasn't to say that she'd never endured long hours on her feet, dealing with the two and a half million things that could go wrong—and did—in the hospitality industry.

But this was different.

Every muscle in her body ached. She was bruised. She was blistered. She could only hope that one day— soon—she'd be calloused.

She'd managed to skewer one thumb repairing saddle stitching and she'd burned the other when she'd tried roasting one of those unidentifiable bricks of meat from the freezer, only to fill the kitchen with smoke caused by its incineration.

She dragged herself out of bed before the sun came up and fell back into it almost as soon as it went back down again.

And through it all, she had to admit that if *she* felt she was working hard, she knew that Russ was working harder because *he* was running two ranches.

He spent every night at the Hopping H, worked side by side with her for a few hours in the morning, went to the Flying J during the midday where she suspected he was bolstering his own strength with food that was more to his liking and his needs, returned in the late afternoon and didn't seem to stop even after he'd sent her into the house, generally on the verge of collapse.

And now it was Friday, exactly two weeks after she'd agreed to this desperate arrangement with Russ, and that evening they were expected back at the Thunder Canyon Resort where Grant and Steph were hosting a reception for them.

Not even the prospect of having the best meal that week was enough to make Melanie want to go there more than she wanted to crawl into bed when Russ called an early day of it.

"I've gotta see to a delivery at my place," he'd told her before he'd left, following an afternoon of tangling with barbed wire fencing and posthole digging.

Considering the ground was pretty frozen, that had been a real walk in the park. She had a fresh set of blisters blooming on her palms, thanks to the experience.

The second he'd driven off in the rattletrap of a pickup truck he'd been driving back and forth between their places all week, she'd hightailed it up to her bathroom and filled the tub with the hottest water the water heater would provide.

He'd told her he would be back to get her by seven.

That meant she could wallow in soothing salts and hot water for a solid hour before she'd even need to think about what to wear to the reception.

Most of her dresses were out of the question, since she had a dozen bruises she preferred to keep covered.

When she gingerly lowered herself into the full tub, her groan echoed around the white tiled walls.

She'd been so busy with Russ that she'd hardly had any time—or energy—to devote to the renovations. She was *supposed* to have had a whirlpool tub installed in the bathroom for the largest bedroom by now. But not even knowing that she could be floating in hot, bubbling water instead of hot, still water was enough to get her too worked up.

She was just too...darned...tired.

She didn't regret for a second experiencing all that she was learning, but she knew—if she were to get her place ready for bookings by February—she couldn't keep up the pace.

She needed hired hands. She needed a foreman to handle them, and everything else related to the actual business of ranching.

She closed her eyes and tilted her head back against the towel she'd folded to use as a pillow. Despite her physical exhaustion, though, her mind was teeming. She needed to talk to Russ about a foreman. Someone trustworthy; someone reliable. Maybe she could persuade him to interview appropriate candidates. And she needed to figure out some sort of program where

her guests could actually have a more hands-on experience with the different kind of chores around the place.

Mucking out stalls was never going to be her favorite
task in the world, but after the better part of two weeks
now, she was getting pretty good at it. And there *was*
something cathartic about that sort of labor.

Her chin sank down another inch. The fragrant water
lapped at her chin. Another few minutes and she'd rinse
off. Take a bracing shower and get cleaned up for the
party.

Another few minutes…

When he drove up to the Hopping H, Russ found the
house dark. Not a single light shined from a single
window.

His first instinct was to make certain that Melanie's
car was still parked in the stand-alone garage behind the
house.

He parked his truck outside the closed doors and,
leaving his headlights shining, he shoved one of the
doors aside.

Her mud-spattered little roadster grinned back at
him from its cozy sanctuary.

Arm braced against the door, Russ lowered his head.
God, he did *not* need this. He didn't need to be running
his life from both ends the way he was. Here at the H.
Home at the Flying J.

Mostly, though, he didn't need knowing that the
sight of her car sitting right where it belonged had relief
running thick and sticky through his veins.

The night Nola had walked out on him, she'd taken
their toddler with her. The only thing Melanie could

try to take was the half of the Hopping H she'd promised him.

And that was the only reason he was relieved to see that car. *Had* to be.

He closed the garage door again, shut off his own vehicle, dousing the headlights, and went in through the kitchen door. "Melanie?" He flicked on the overhead light and the kitchen sprang into view.

He might moan about all the changes she'd made to the place, but the kitchen was pretty much a showplace. He'd seen catalogs of setups that didn't look this swell. There was no wasted space and despite the granite and stainless "high-end" look that Melanie often referred to, there didn't seem to him to be anything unnecessary, either. It was all useful. There were no gewgaws cluttering up the place.

And though he'd rather spit nails than admit it, the comparisons he couldn't help but draw between the H's newfangled kitchen and his own weren't too flattering in his favor.

"Melanie!" With the light from the kitchen guiding his way, he stomped across the subfloor that Melanie's contractors had put down in the great room the previous day. Before long, there would be reclaimed planks laid atop it, and once that was finished, the walls would get a fresh coat of paint and some of Melanie's specially ordered furniture could begin coming in.

"Melanie." He started up the stairs that he'd insisted be bordered off by some sort of safety feature until the custom balustrades she'd ordered could arrive; and the answer was an ugly, but utilitarian, steel rod. Finally, at the top of the stairs, he saw a light coming from her bedroom.

"I hope you're ready, princess, or we're going to be late." He stopped at her doorway, rapping his knuckles on the opened door. "Hear me?"

When he got no reply, he rubbed his hand down his face. For the past two weeks he'd managed *not* to ever look inside Melanie's bedroom. Not when he finally dragged his sorry ass to sleep where he spent the next few hours tossing in a bed that was about six inches too short for him. And not when he rose a good two hours before she did, so he could at least get a few hours of chores done without her uncommonly distracting presence.

He tilted his head, looking around the door into the room.

She didn't have to worry about her bed being too short. The massive sleigh bed looked as if it could double as a passenger liner.

She wasn't much of a housekeeper, either, he decided, looking at the rumpled patchwork quilt and pillows that were falling off onto the floor. There was a laundry basket full of clothes sitting by the closet door, another pile of clothes sitting in the corner, and paint brochures littered the top of the dresser, alongside a hairbrush and a fancy glass perfume bottle.

No sign of Melanie, though.

He ducked his head back out of the room, dragging his eyes away from where they wanted to linger on that long, wide, bed. Two doors down was the bathroom that they had to share, and the door was ajar there, too, though there was no light shining from inside.

He grimaced. Where the hell was she?

He continued down the floor, flipping on lights in each room, looking inside, turning the lights back off. He even looked in his *own* room.

As if she'd have ever stepped foot in there. Outside of his dreams, that was.

Was it any wonder that he was sleeping as few hours as humanly possible?

He strode back down the hall, stuck his head into the bathroom and flipped the light on in there, not expecting to see anything more than he'd seen in the half-dozen empty bedrooms.

But, holy hell, he *did* see. And plenty.

A splash of water as she jerked with the light that shined brightly down on her damp head, a tangle of long, ivory limbs that scrambled to find footing as she started to push up out of the tub, only to realize that doing so made matters even worse, and she sank back down into the water, dragging the towel from behind her head right into the sudsy water to spread frantically over her torso.

But it was too late.

The water wasn't *that* sudsy and he'd seen more than enough to guarantee more sleepless nights.

"*What* are you doing?" Her shaking voice was just shy of a shriek as it bounced around the tiled room.

"Looking for you." He shot back the cuff of his white shirt—the dressiest he was ever likely to get—and made a point of looking at his sturdy wristwatch. "It's nearly seven."

She groaned, covering her face with her hand. "Turn around!"

He started to grin, but her painful embarrassment

was palpable. "It's a little late for that," he couldn't resist offering, but he did turn around.

Only that gave him a view of the mirror over the sink, through which he could see her reflection as she gingerly rose from the tub. The soaked towel she held protectively around her might have covered the essentials, but that still left plenty of long, slender legs exposed, and the side of her hip.

"Damn." He spun back around, startling her into another splash that sent water cascading over the side of the claw-footed tub onto his boots.

"I said turn around!" She practically shrank back against the wall beside the tub. Her hands scrabbled against his as he reached for the towel. "What do you think you're doing?"

"Good God," he muttered. She was more skittish than a new filly. "Relax. If I wanted to cop a feel, you'd know it." He pressed the towel flat against her belly, allowing her some modesty while he nudged the soaked terry cloth away from her side. "Where the hell did *that* come from?"

The bruise stretched from her rib cage down to the provocative swell of her hip.

She was still pushing aside his hands. "Who knows? Around the tenth time I knocked into the rail around the riding arena? Or maybe the twentieth time I pulled a saddle down off its hook? I've always bruised easily."

There was nothing easy-looking about the bruise. Everything from indigo to yellow was splotched across her side. "You should see a doctor."

"Do *you* go whining to a doctor every time you get a bruise?" She yanked the side of the towel around her hip, enveloping herself more fully as she awkwardly stepped over the high side of the old-fashioned tub. "Somehow I *really* doubt it." She kept one hand holding the dripping towel above her breasts and the other holding the sides together over her rear as she sidled out into the hall.

"Yeah, well, I'm used to crap like this." He followed her right into her disheveled bedroom. "You're not."

"And what do you think a doctor would do? Prescribe an ice pack? Last thing I need to be is more of a laughingstock in this town."

He let out a hard breath. "You're not a laughingstock. You're dripping water everywhere."

"So, it'll be just one more thing I need to clean up. And don't even *think* about pointing out what a miserable job I've been doing on that score, too, because I am well aware of what a mess things have become. Now, would you *please* get out of here so I can get dressed?"

"I can call and cancel."

"It's much too late for that. It'd be unforgivably rude."

"As opposed to our being late?"

"Fashionably late." She seemed to give up the notion of him leaving to afford her some privacy and yanked open the closet door. Still struggling to keep the towel around her, she rifled through a few hangers, then yanked out two, tossing the garments onto her bed.

"Dammit, you've got a bruise on the back of your thigh, too."

She pulled the back of the towel down, covering the mark. "I have them all over. Do you want to catalog them?"

"Do I need to?" He wasn't exactly joking, and damned if it had nothing to do with that annoying urge he couldn't get rid of to put his hands on her body. All *over* her body.

"I was being facetious," she pointed out.

Big surprise. "I wasn't."

Giving him an annoyed look when he still stood there, she stomped over to the big pine dresser. It was rustic in the original sense, not because it had been designed to look rough and old, and when she pulled at the top drawer, it stuck. Muttering under her breath, she yanked again, only to grab the knot in her towel when it slipped precariously. She had a bruise on the underside of her upper arm. Much smaller than the others, but just as purple. And another on her shin.

"Need some help?"

"No." She grabbed the drawer handle again and gave a fast yank.

The drawer slid free and right out of its runners.

"Dammit!" The drawer fell out of her hand. She barely managed to jump back before it crashed to the floor in a showering explosion of panties. "Are you satisfied now?"

There were tears in her eyes, turning the brown to a soft, mossy green. He remembered all too well the way Nola had used her tears as a tool in her arsenal. But Melanie looked away, giving her cheeks a surreptitious swipe. She stepped out of the pile of underwear and went over to the laundry basket in the corner, unearthing a robe.

Acting as if he weren't in the room at all, she kept her back to him as she whipped the thin black fabric around her shoulders, allowing the soaked towel to fall to her feet from beneath it. She tied the robe at her waist, snatched up the towel and walked out of the bedroom.

Russ looked down at the array of lingerie littered practically at his feet. Sighing, he hunkered down and began gathering them up, rapidly tossing the laces and satins and silks back into the drawer.

"You don't have to do that." Melanie was back, her eyes still that murky shade of green. She knelt down, scooping the long folds of the robe around her legs, and waved at his hands as if she were shooing away a fly.

He dropped his handful of lacy white scraps in her palm. "Well," he murmured, "at least you've got plenty of panties that you *could* wear."

The flush began in her neck and ran all the way up into her cheeks. "The comedic world doesn't know what it's missing without you." Knees on the floor, she bent forward, reaching past him, swallowing a silky-looking triangle of black fabric and ribbon in her fist. She sat back and tossed the minuscule thong into the jumbled mess now inside the drawer once more. She rose, but he picked up the drawer before she could and slid it back into place in the dresser.

"Thank you." She didn't look at him. Her cheeks were still red, and he knew what a dog he was when he wondered just how far that flush spread down her torso.

"You've never cried before." The words came out before he thought to stop them. "Not in front of me. Not once these past two weeks. No matter what I threw at you." And he'd thrown plenty. He'd made her work as hard or harder than he would have expected any hired hand to work. And while being the owner of a small ranch usually meant being the one to pull the hardest duties, he hadn't given her much of a break being new to it all.

Maybe that was why he felt like a bastard seeing those bruises on her silky white skin. Because he might as well have put them there himself.

He put his hand under her chin, gently lifting until he could see into her face. "But you'll cry over spilled panties."

"I am *not* crying." Her voice was husky.

He ran his thumb slowly up her cheek toward the corner of her eye. "Really." He caught the teardrop before it could join the previous one whose trail he'd just followed.

Her lashes fluttered down. Thick. Soft. Dark. The way they were every day, in and out, start to finish. "Could have fooled me." He left his hand there, feeling the delicate arch of her cheekbone, the flutter of her pulse beneath the fine edge of her jaw. His big hand looked clumsy, rough, against her perfectly smooth, flawless complexion. "It's not a crime."

The assurance surprised even him. He'd inured himself to women's tears more than ten years ago when he'd learned just how treacherously they could be used against him.

"No. It's just weak."

He sighed faintly. Her black robe clung to her lithe figure even more than that soaked towel had. "You're not weak."

"I don't need platitudes from you."

"Have I bothered with them before?"

She blinked, her gaze skipping up to his, then away. "No. You're…annoyingly frank."

"Then why would I start now? It's been a hell of a few weeks. *I'm* tired, and I'm used to this kind of physical grind."

"You work harder than anyone I've ever seen."

"Is that condemnation or praise?" he asked wryly.

The flush was finally fading, leaving her cheek cooler beneath his fingers. She sucked in her upper lip for a moment. "Maybe a bit of both," she admitted. Her lashes lifted, but her gaze skittered away from his yet again.

"Then let me annoy you some more." He tilted her chin up another inch. "You are many things, Melanie McFarlane, but weak is not one of them."

And then, because he *was* weak, he lowered his head and slowly rubbed his lips across hers.

She jerked, going ramrod still. But she didn't pull away. And when common sense finally penetrated the fog clouding his brain and he lifted his head, her eyes were no longer wet with tears.

They were just filled with a wary confusion that he recognized all too well.

Because he felt the very same damn thing.

He lowered his hand. Took a step back. Softly cleared his throat. "If we're gonna go, we'd better—"

"—go soon. Yes." She moistened her lips, taking a step back, also. Her hands tightened the sash of her robe. "Give me t-ten minutes."

He figured it would more likely be at least twice that. But he nodded and finally backed toward the door of her bedroom. "Next time you take a soak, use Epsom salts. Good for taking the aches out. There're a couple of cartons in the tack room."

She nodded. "Okay."

He took another step back, managed to bump his ass right into the doorjamb. "Okay."

Her head bobbed. "Okay."

Then she flushed a little all over again, probably realizing—like he was—just how idiotic they sounded. "I'll be downstairs." He pulled the door shut behind him.

He leaned his forehead against the wall, standing there in the dim hallway for a long minute.

He felt as if he'd just run a marathon.

How the hell was he supposed to last for five and a half more months of this?

Chapter Nine

Melanie stared at the collection of wrapped gifts piled high on the linen-draped table situated near the stone-fronted fireplace in the beautifully elegant Gallatin Room. It was the finest restaurant in the Thunder Canyon Resort, with a spectacular view of the snow-covered slopes, but when she and Russ arrived after their awkwardly silent drive from the Hopping H, she certainly didn't expect to find that the establishment had been closed for the little "get-together" that Grant and his fiancée were hosting for them.

But the proof had been there in the thick velvety rope draped across the entrance. An ivory placard with black script hung from the rope. *Closed for private party.*

"I can't believe they closed the restaurant for us," Melanie had whispered to Russ.

"I can't believe you were actually ready in ten minutes," he'd returned.

"Do you even get it? It's a Friday evening terribly close to Christmas. The mountain is ripe with snowpack and the resort is probably close to capacity. Do you know what kind of till this place would have?"

"It's Grant's decision," Russ had reminded. "I'd rather have had this thing over at the Hitching Post where I wouldn't have to worry about using the wrong damn fork, but this is his territory now."

And then the man in question had spotted them and ushered them inside the elegant restaurant where Melanie had noticed two things.

The restaurant was nearly full of people she'd maybe seen once or twice since she'd moved to Thunder Canyon. And that banquet table next to the snapping, crackling, fragrant fire was nearly bowing beneath the weight of wedding gifts piled on top of it.

"You guys really shouldn't have," Russ was saying. He, too, was staring at the gift display with some chagrin.

"We considered starting to open them for you since you two were late." Lizbeth Stanton grinned audaciously. She was hanging on to the arm of Mitchell Cates, who Melanie knew was president of a farm and ranch equipment company. "We just figured you were busy doing the newlywed thing."

"Don't mind her," Mitchell said, quietly, though his dark eyes were smiling, too, particularly when he looked down adoringly at the curvaceously petite woman. "She's just anxious to reach that stage herself."

Everyone laughed, and Lizbeth rolled her eyes, looking good-natured. "That's only because I've finally found the right man with whom I should be a newlywed. Who knew all I had to do was stop looking?" She unwound Mitchell's arm from her shoulder and came up to Melanie, offering an enthusiastic hug and kiss on the cheek. "I hope you two will be very happy." Lizbeth practically bounced to Russ. "And *you,* you cantankerous devil. I'll even wish you congratulations."

Russ hugged the girl in return, though his gaze was on Mitch. "Did I miss something?"

Lizbeth's smile was so wide it practically lit the well-planned shadows that accentuated the Gallatin Room's elegant intimacy. She lifted her left hand, waving it around for all to see the glittering diamond ring on her finger. "And, *yes,* for all of you doubting Thomases," she gave Russ an arch look that was nevertheless full of merriment, "this ring is going to stay right where it is."

"That is, until I put a wedding band on that finger, as well," Mitchell added.

"No kidding? Hell, man. When did this happen?" Russ lifted his arm off Melanie's shoulder and shook the other man's hand.

"More 'n a month ago," Mitch said, seeming to surprise everyone. "Lizbeth was the one who wanted to wait to announce it."

The young woman brushed back a sheaf of the kind of luxuriously thick hair that Melanie had always envied. "It wasn't that I was uncertain," she offered, looking serious for a moment.

Mitch ran his finger down her cheek. "I know."

"Well." Russ still looked surprised, but then so did

most of the other people present. "Congratulations." He pumped Mitch's hand again, then nudged Lizbeth under the chin and dropped a kiss on her forehead. "I never thought I'd see the day, but it looks like you've got things right, kiddo. I'm happy for you."

"We're really not trying to steal your thunder," Lizbeth returned sincerely. "I just couldn't keep quiet about it for a minute longer."

"There's a surprise," Dax Traub commented wryly. Melanie had heard the broodingly handsome man had been briefly engaged to Lizbeth, but it didn't look to her as if there were any hard feelings between them. Particularly since he had a stylish blonde on his arm—Shandie Solomon, whom she recognized from the hair salon she'd scouted out when she'd first come to Thunder Canyon—and they couldn't keep their besotted eyes off one another.

If Melanie had to make a guess, she figured it was extremely safe to say that she and Russ were probably the *only* people present who weren't head-over-heels crazy for their date that night.

Though, as she found herself in an impromptu sort of receiving line as Russ's friends all passed by offering introductions where needed along with their seemingly sincere best wishes, she couldn't pretend that she wasn't feeling pretty topsy-turvy since Russ had found her sleeping in the bathtub. With one portion of her mind occupied with returning hugs and giving appropriate responses, the rest of her was still mortified about that entire fiasco.

She was more unnerved, however, by the crazy sense that she could still taste him on her lips.

His kiss had been completely unexpected.

Completely inappropriate.

Completely…unforgettable.

And maybe, if she had an ounce of real experience to fall back on when it came to men, she'd have some idea of whether Russ felt one iota of the same confusion she'd felt. Because, goodness knew, there was not a sign of anything on his rugged face or in his demeanor. And she'd tried to find some hint, studying him surreptitiously the entire time it had taken them to drive from the Hopping H to the resort.

Finally, he'd just sardonically asked if he'd had some sort of stain on his shirt or something.

She'd sweetly replied that she was just shocked over his clothing. She hadn't thought he'd owned anything but blue jeans, and the fine black wool trousers he wore with his highly polished boots and white button-down shirt were a shock.

Better that he think she was a snob than that he see just how shaken she'd actually been. And still was, if she were honest with herself.

Steph and Grant were the last to greet them. "Here." Steph pushed a glass of wine into Melanie's hand. "You look like you need a little fortification. What's this guy doing? Wearing you out already?"

Melanie managed not to jump when Russ dropped his arm over her shoulder once more. "The Hopping H is keeping us both pretty busy," she admitted.

Through the soft knit jersey of her long-sleeved black top, Russ's fingers felt warm where they swirled over her shoulder. "That's one way of putting it." His voice was lazy. Full of innuendo.

Predictably, Melanie's face warmed. She focused on Grant. "Closing the Gallatin just for us was far too generous of you, Grant."

"Nothing's too good for an old friend like Russ," he assured, giving Russ a look she couldn't quite interpret, though his voice was perfectly smooth. "Now, let's have a seat before the chef gets any more testy about delaying his dinner service." He gestured toward the tables that had been fashioned banquet-style into a sort of U-shape. "You two are at the head, of course." He tucked his hand at the small of Steph's back and lifted his own wineglass in a toast as everyone settled themselves around the tables. "I don't know who it was that said it, but I can personally attest that it's true." His gaze went to his fiancée for a moment before he focused back on Russ. "The most precious possession that ever comes to a man in this world is a woman's heart. Guard it well, my friend." His smile widened, taking in Melanie, as well. "Here is to both of you. Melanie and Russ. We all wish you both nothing but happiness."

With everyone lifting their glasses to them, Melanie had never felt like such a fraud. Beneath the fine flaxen-colored linen draping the table, Russ's hand closed over the fists she'd made of hers in her lap.

"All right, then," Marshall Cates added. He was Mitchell Cates' brother. When Russ introduced them, he'd said the man was a sports doctor, which had struck her as appropriate, given the man's athletic looks. "What we really want to see is a kiss. Wouldn't everyone agree?"

"Marshall," Mia, his wife, chided, shyly humorous.

Her long black hair gleamed from the firelight flickering behind her. "Don't embarrass them."

"That's what Russ gets for taking off to Las Vegas to get hitched. We didn't get to see the ceremony. Least we can see is a kiss."

"He's just egging on Russ because he whipped Marsh's butt last month at poker," Dax drawled, grinning. "Speaking of which," he looked at Russ and Melanie, "your new bride *does* know you're going to have to take a powder every now and again for a couple rounds of cards, doesn't she?"

"Knows all about it," Russ assured so confidently that Melanie couldn't help but wonder what else he was adept at lying about. "As for a kiss—"

The only warning Melanie had was in the squeeze he gave her hands beneath the tablecloth just before he leaned closer to her and caught her lips with his.

A burst of laughter and clapping surrounded them, but Melanie barely heard. Then Russ shifted, their lips parting, and he whispered in her ear. *"Smile."*

Like a mindless doll, she smiled.

Inside however, she was quaking. Could his fingers touching the inside of her wrists feel her racing pulse?

Fortunately, the wait staff was suddenly there, delivering chilled plates filled with their starter salads. Everyone's attention was no longer pointed directly at them as Melanie extricated her hands from Russ's grip.

"We won't stay long," he murmured.

"It's all right." These were his friends. And it surprised her that she wished that, some day, they might be her friends, too.

She wasn't in Thunder Canyon to make friends. She

was there to prove herself to her family. Once and for all.

But somehow, the reminder fell flat during the very excellent meal that followed. She even managed to shake off some of her bone-deep tiredness somewhere along the way. From the jicama and carrot slaw starter to the entrée of smoked duck with risotto, Melanie couldn't find a single fault either in taste or presentation.

It was no wonder the Gallatin Room had the stellar reputation that it did.

Russ tilted his head toward hers. "Enjoying the meal?"

"If I was still running McFarlane House Atlanta, I'd make a serious attempt at stealing the head chef," she admitted, though what she was enjoying even more than the meal was the easy camaraderie between Russ and their guests. It was like nothing she'd ever before experienced.

She'd always been either the boss's daughter or the lame-duck boss. She'd never been part of a group of friends like this; they seemed to squabble almost as much as they laughed. The ribbing that Russ took ranged from giving up his cherished bachelorhood to his vocal dislike for all things new. But he also gave back as good as he got and never seemed to take anything too personally.

"What *do* you plan to do about a cook?" he persisted.

She drew her mind back to the topic in question. "Hire one." She made a wry grimace. "Once I can figure out how to fit in time to take interviews, that is." When she'd been planning to buy Grant Clifton's place, she'd hoped that Stephanie's mother, Marie, would stay on in her position as cook. But that was all water under the bridge, now.

"Ever think you don't need to do it all?"

She looked at the other guests, all enjoying their meal and the company, if the half-dozen lively conversations going on around them were any indication. "I used to be the queen of delegating."

"Bet you didn't get bruises the size of Montana all over your body when you did so."

"Not visible ones," she murmured, earning herself a searching look from him. But whatever he would have said was derailed by Steph.

"Hey there, lovebirds," she said. "Cut the whispering so you can cut the cake, instead." She gestured to the table that two waiters were rolling into the room.

Melanie's jaw loosened a little at the sight of the two-tiered wedding cake perched on the cart. It was a spectacular creation in white icing with ivory rosebuds completely filling the space between the tiers. More buds, tightly packed into a dome shape, seemed to bloom right out of the top layer. "Oh, my goodness."

"Damn, Grant," Russ said. "I hope you're not planning on sending me a bill for all this. I'd have to sell the Flying J."

Grant chuckled. "Blame this one on Steph."

"Every bride should have a wedding cake to cut into and share," she said. "Somehow, I suspect there wasn't much of one on that quick trip you made to Vegas."

She smiled right at Melanie and her throat suddenly ached. From her father, she received offers to arrange an annulment. From this young woman—

more acquaintance than anything, really—she received *this*.

Russ stood, and held back her chair. The hand he used to help her rise probably looked solicitous, but Melanie knew it was because of the bruises he'd seen. And she was grateful, because she'd become impossibly stiff sitting through dinner. "What about every groom?" he asked.

"Grooms get the wedding night," Steph returned with a laugh.

Grant gave her a sidelong look. "I'll remind you of that."

Steph's impish grin just widened. "I would hope so."

"Get a room," Dax suggested dryly.

"That might be just how this whole thing started," Grant pondered aloud, eyeing Russ and Melanie. "With a room."

Not exactly, Melanie thought, as she moved with Russ to the trolley carrying the cake. She blamed her odd sense of wistfulness on exhaustion.

"Here you go, Mrs. Chilton." The thin young waiter handed her a long, pearl-handled cake knife.

Mrs. Chilton. They'd signed that marriage certificate two weeks ago, but it was the first time since then that someone had addressed her so. A glance up at Russ gave her nothing in return but his once-more typically impassive look.

"Come on, Russ. You know the drill. Put your hand on top of hers and cut a slice of cake," Lizbeth prompted when they seemed to hesitate too long.

A glint of humor shined suddenly in Russ's eyes. "You catching all this?" he asked Mitch.

"Taking notes, my friend," the other man returned, easily. "Taking notes."

Melanie could feel Russ's body heat burning through her top and narrow silk slacks as he moved more closely behind her and reached around, covering her hand with his. She felt surrounded by him and couldn't seem to stop the fine tremors from shaking through her, but his hand seemed rock-steady. Beneath their combined touch, the knife slid smoothly once, then twice, through the slightly pearlescent buttercream enveloping the first layer. She removed the slice and slid it onto the silver-rimmed plate the waiter handed her, then looked hesitantly up at Russ.

"You use your fingers, princess," he murmured, his lips twitching.

She picked up a moist chunk of the white cake. "I am well aware of that."

"Think she's going to smash it into his face?" she heard someone ask behind them.

She lifted her eyebrow, watching Russ. "Maybe I should," she warned, keeping her voice light.

"You could always try," he offered blandly.

Of course, she had no real desire to shove cake against his face. Maybe once, she would have. But not after the past few weeks.

She lifted the bite-size piece to his mouth and slipped it past his lips. Feeling breathless, she started to lower her hand as he swallowed the confection, but he circled her wrist. His thumb seemed to press right against her pulse as he slowly sucked the icing from the tips of her thumb and forefinger.

He'd felt her pulse leap that time for certain.

"Is it getting hot in here?" another voice asked, and everyone laughed again.

Russ finally released Melanie's hand and she buried it in the linen napkin the waiter supplied. It definitely *was* hot. She felt as if she were melting from the inside out.

"Open up," Russ murmured, holding his piece for her, in return.

Melanie moistened her lips nervously, then opened them. He nudged the cake inside and slowly dragged his thumb against the edge of her teeth as he drew his hand away.

She barely tasted the cake as she swallowed. His brown eyes looked nearly black in the soft light of the restaurant and she couldn't seem to pull her gaze away from them.

Then his thumb touched the corner of her mouth. "Frosting," he murmured in the half moment before his mouth came down over hers. She felt the tip of his tongue touch the same spot his thumb had, before it flicked wickedly, briefly, against her lower lip.

All too quickly, he was lifting his head again and she was grateful for the arm he slid around her shoulder as he turned back to face their guests. If it weren't for him holding her, she feared her shaking knees might well have given out after that impossibly brief, impossibly searing kiss.

She was vaguely aware of the waiters taking over the cake table as they swiftly cut and began passing out slices to all the guests, including her and Russ.

He tucked right in to his, giving her a sideways look. "Cake'll never be the same again," he murmured, then took his first bite.

Feeling utterly parched, she reached for her wine-glass and polished off the remains.

She was beginning to fear very much that it wasn't only cake that would never be the same.

Chapter Ten

The drive back to the Hopping H after the party was silent, except for the squeaks and rattles from the classic pickup truck Russ had picked up for a song a few weeks ago.

He'd figured it would take him about three months to get his Chevy restored to its former glory, but when he'd planned on that, he hadn't been hitched to Melanie McFarlane.

Instead, the only thing he'd managed to do with the vehicle since he'd agreed to Melanie's proposition was cover the torn seat upholstery with a striped wool blanket, and change the carburetor.

He had other trucks he could have been driving the past few weeks. Ones that were further along in the restoration process. Ones that were worth a pretty penny, in fact, to the folks who'd eventually pick them up from him.

He'd expected Melanie to turn her nose up at riding in the rundown vehicle. To insist on taking her expensive little Porsche if they went somewhere together.

But she hadn't turned up that narrow, patrician nose of hers. She hadn't refused or insisted or sneered.

She'd just stretched her long leg—clad in some shiny black silky pants that made them look even longer— up onto the running board and climbed inside. The only wince that had crossed her features seemed to have come from her aching muscles.

The lights of the resort were no longer visible in his rearview mirror. His dashboard didn't have any working lights, but there was enough illumination from the silver moon hanging low on the horizon for him to see the gleam of her auburn hair above the turned-up collar of her hip-length leather coat. She was so silent, he might have thought she'd fallen asleep, but he knew she hadn't even before she lifted her hand wearing that cheap wedding ring and tucked her hair behind her ear.

She glanced at him and in the darkness, her eyes seemed more mysterious than ever.

He shouldn't have kissed her.

Not back at the house. Not at the reception.

Not ever.

They had an agreement. Hell, even now the napkin on which they'd outlined their terms was folded up and tucked in his back pocket. He carried it as a reminder of all that he stood to gain.

Only now, it was also a reminder of all that he'd promised *not* to do.

No hanky-panky.

Which was the only thing he seemed able to focus his brain on lately.

"I don't know what we're going to do with all of those gifts." Her voice was soft.

The gifts in question were loaded in the truck bed, unopened and covered with his canvas tarp. "Open 'em like we're expected to."

"It seems wrong to accept them."

"Would you rather have pushed them back in everyone's faces tonight?"

"No. Of course not." She needlessly tucked her hair behind her ear again. "Your friends are very nice."

"They're all right." He drummed his thumb against the steering wheel. Couldn't seem to drum away the feel of her lips, though.

Full. Soft. Warm.

Since he was thinking about the feel of them, his mind naturally went on to the taste of them.

The taste of her.

"Kind of like most families, I guess," he added doggedly, shoving the memories, the thoughts, the damned imagination, into a mental lockbox. "We get along. Don't get along. But you keep hanging together in the end, no matter what. Still can't believe Lizbeth and Mitch, though."

"Why?"

"She's had marriage on her mind for so long, it didn't seem to matter much *who* the groom was."

"She looks devoted to Mitch."

"Yeah. Think maybe she is." For him it was quite a concession. "I sure in hell hope so, anyway."

"He's about your age, isn't he?"

"Two years younger 'n me. Your age, actually." He watched her from the corner of his eye. Sometimes he found it difficult to believe she was thirty. Underneath that privileged air she had about her there was something distinctly…innocent. And it puzzled—no, it *intrigued* the hell out of him. "And Lizbeth—she's just a kid."

"She's petite," Melanie allowed, "but she didn't look like a teenager to me. And Stephanie's pretty young, too, I'm guessing."

"Yeah, but there's a world of difference between Steph and Lizbeth. Steph's known responsibility for a long while now. And Lizbeth, well she's not always kept her nose to the straight and narrow. She's twenty-three…no, she's twenty-four now. Not exactly a teenager, true. But still—" He shook his head, still finding the matchup surprising.

"If your son is ten years old, you must have been younger than that when *you* were married."

His scalp abruptly tightened and the problem seemed set to spread through the rest of him. It took an effort to keep his hand on the wheel loose and easy. "Twenty-one. And I was too young." Knowing it in hindsight didn't do much to change the painful result, though. He still had a son he hadn't seen in three years.

"And your…ex-wife?" She seemed to be treading warily.

"She was twenty-one, also." He slid his jaw to one side. Back again. "Nola." Then he wished he'd just kept his mouth shut because Melanie lifted her knee onto the seat, angling slightly to face him more squarely.

More openly.

There were a few things he wanted open between them, but discussion about his failure of a marriage, his failure as a father, was not one of them.

"Was she from Thunder Canyon, too?"

"No. *Hell,* no."

She made a soft sound. "Let me guess. Boston."

He didn't answer.

"How did you meet?"

A bloody fluke, he thought, and had no intention of answering. But the words were all of a sudden just coming out of his damn fool mouth. "She was driving through from Canada with college friends. Had car trouble on the highway. I was on my way back from Idaho, towing a truck I'd picked up over there."

"What kind of truck?"

"Sixty-nine Chevy Stepside."

She looked blank.

"An old pickup."

"You seem to like them a lot," she offered.

Back to safer territory, he patted the steering wheel. "There's always more life in one of these old girls than a person thinks." He shot Melanie a look. "I restore them."

The realization made her "Ah," sound more than a little relieved. Maybe she thought he was cash-poor or something.

"It's a hobby, then?"

"I guess." He enjoyed the work. Found it satisfying in the same way he found rounding up an ornery cow satisfying. And over the years, he'd earned back a fair chunk of change. But he'd never been in it for the money.

"I've never had a hobby," she murmured.

He snorted. "*Every*one has a hobby, even if it's collecting string. My grandmother, she had big ol' balls of string in her closet. She did the same with foil. Wouldn't throw the stuff away for love nor money."

"Only thing I'm collecting these days are bruises."

Wasn't that the truth. But thinking about the marks on her silky flesh led back down dangerous paths. One path was marked Insane Desire in big flaming letters. The other path just had a half-burned wood sign saying Guilty SOB.

He flexed his fingers again on the steering wheel. "What about when you were a kid? You probably had the most expensive dolls money could buy."

She seemed to think about it. "I had a miniature of our flagship hotel in Philadelphia. You know—one of those big doll houses. Only this one was a hotel."

"What'd you do with it?"

"Nothing. It sat on a fancy stand in my bedroom."

"You never did *anything* with it?" They reached the turnoff to the Hopping H and he slowed down, giving her a surprised look as he took the turn. "Stuck your Barbies or G.I. Joe's together in a room where they played doctor?"

She gave a soft exclamation. "No. But that's an interesting glimpse into the kind of games *you* must have played as a boy."

He grinned. "When it came to playing doctor, I didn't bother acting it out with damn dolls. There was this girl in my second-grade class. I'll never forget her. Long red braids. Freckled face. Round gold glasses always sliding down her nose. Oh, I had it bad for little

Mary Pendleton. And she didn't find *me* too odious."
His voice dropped, repeating the term Melanie had
applied to him that night at Grant's Christmas party.
"But she moved away from Thunder Canyon the summer after that year. Broke my heart and never bothered
to look back." Maybe that's where his stupid weakness
for red-haired women had begun.

"Poor baby," she murmured.

"What about you? Who was your first crush?"

She shook her head, looking away from him. "This
is silly."

"Just like a woman," he goaded. "I bare my soul and
you—"

"Mason Tolliver the Third."

"The Third. Sounds repressed."

She gave a half laugh. "Don't be mean. He was wonderful, actually. He was the son of our sous chef and
we used to tear around the hotel, getting into all sorts
of mischief for two eight-year-olds."

"No kidding." He tried to imagine it in his head, but
couldn't really come close. He'd grown up on a ranch.
What he knew of chefs and fancy hotels was pretty
damn minimal.

"Until his father moved on to become executive chef
with one of our competitors," she continued. "And that
was that." She lifted her hand. Let it fall back in her lap.

"Who came after The Third?"

She made a soft *hmm*. "Nobody, really. I went to
boarding school shortly after that. All girls. After I graduated, I started working for my father at our flagship
hotel."

"College?"

"Private," she answered immediately.

"Naturally," he commented, tongue-in-cheek. "Is there any other kind?" Like the community college or university extensions through which he'd gotten his degrees.

"I went where my parents sent me."

He eyed her. "How dutiful. Must have been *some* shenanigans in there somewhere."

She merely smiled, not answering.

Which just had his imagination running all over hell and gone again.

He gunned the engine, taking the last hill that led up to the Hopping H's main house. After having driven the road so many times back and forth between his place lately, he could have driven it with his eyes closed. Though he did notice that the tires didn't grip quite as well as they should. "You'll want to get this hill regraded in the next year or so."

"It's already on my list of improvements." She hesitated for a moment. "Does, um, does your son live with his mother?"

Just that quickly, his nerves tightened all over again, and it was as if they'd never shared a smile, much less any sort of civilized conversation. "Do you see my boy living here with me? Trust a woman to keep poking where she doesn't belong."

The knee slid off the bench seat and once again, she was facing firmly forward. "Don't worry." Her voice was as cool as the silvery gleam of moonlight on the snow. "I can assure you it won't happen again."

He let out a long breath. "You're an annoying woman."

"Fitting." Her tongue seemed to snap off her *T*s. "You are an annoying man."

If they were sniping at each other, it was easier to remember why his good ol' buddies Hanky and Panky had no business coming for a visit—no matter how briefly.

He pulled up in front of the house, stopping short enough that the tires skidded on the gravel.

She looked over at him when he didn't turn off the engine. "Are you going to go off and sulk now?" She huffed slightly, not waiting for an answer. "Never mind." She reached for the door handle, having to give it a pretty good yank to make it move. Then she slid out of the truck, and stomped up the wide steps and through the front door.

He heard the slam of it even above the truck's engine.

"Annoying woman," he muttered again and shoved the truck in gear, wheeling it around in a wide circle.

He'd sleep under his own damn roof where nobody picked and probed at wounds that were better left hidden from the light of day.

Melanie stood next to the big picture window in the darkened great room, and watched the taillights of Russ's truck disappear back down the hill.

She pressed her forehead to the cold glass pane and wished that she'd kept her increasingly insatiable curiosity about the man to herself.

Maybe if she hadn't dared to ask him more about his son, he wouldn't have driven away as if he couldn't get away from her quickly enough.

She'd expected the evening to be an awful experience. Something that had to be endured.

But once she'd managed to put aside her sense of

guilt for misleading all of those people, she'd enjoyed herself. Enjoyed the company.

You enjoyed Russ's company, the voice inside her head taunted her.

Turning away from that truth as well as the window, she unfastened her coat and hung it on the rack by the door. Shivering a little in the coolness of the house, she headed for the stairs. Each step up was an exercise in fresh muscle aches and if she hadn't been afraid that she wouldn't get back up again, she would have sat right down on the treads midway up to have a rest.

In her bedroom, she tried not to think about what had happened there earlier. Of course, the more she tried not to think, the more she *did,* so basically she was tormented whatever she did.

She finally dragged the quilt off the tumbled bed, carried it along with a pillow back downstairs where she stuck a long match in the wood that Russ had placed in the fireplace from the stack of wood he'd arranged to be delivered. It was stacked now in the storage building off the side of the house that she intended, eventually, to refit into a covered hot tub and sauna.

The flame immediately began licking up through the brittle kindling and she tossed the match into the flame, set the metal fire screen back in place and gingerly lowered herself onto the long, overstuffed couch that had also been delivered this past week. The matching pieces, unfortunately, were still missing in action.

But for now, the couch felt wonderful. The flame in the fireplace snapped and crackled as it worked at the split logs and she felt a little warmer just from the comforting sounds. She managed to peel down the zippers of her spiked-heel boots, then she fell back against the couch and let the boots fall where they would.

With the soft bed pillow hugged to her aching side, she dragged the quilt over herself and stretched out on the long couch.

She'd known all along that Russ Chilton was an annoying man. A perplexing, thoroughly disturbing, annoying man.

She shifted again, seeking a more comfortable position. Finally, she ended up flat on her back, her arms stretched up over her head, resting over the arm of the couch.

Who was he to probe into her history, only to go all taciturn on her again when she asked about his? It wasn't as if *she* had a child who was completely absent. Was it any wonder she was curious? And who was he to take out on her whatever issues he had with his family?

She had plenty of issues with her own family. She wasn't making someone else the scapegoat of them.

No, you only married a stranger to keep from confronting those issues.

She stared up into the shadows of the high, wood-beamed ceiling with that taunting voice circling truthfully inside her head and nearly screamed when she heard a footfall right beside her. She sat bolt upright, grabbing the pillow in her hands as if it were any sort of useful weapon, and nearly collapsed again at the sharp pain that had her crying out loud.

Hunched over, her arm wrapped across her ribs as if that would help the pain, she peered at Russ. "What are you doing here?" Her tone was hardly welcoming.

He exhaled noisily, and dumped his armload of

wrapped wedding gifts onto the end of the couch. "Playing husband to an ungrateful wife."

She'd forgotten all about the gifts in the back of the pickup truck. "I'm not ungrateful," she defended tightly. Just a thoroughly self-involved, spoiled woman.

"Would you prefer shrew?"

She threw her pillow at him only to gasp again.

He caught the pillow and tossed it aside. "That's it. Come on." He grabbed the quilt and threw it around her shoulders. Before she could blink, she found herself swaddled in patchworked blues and lifted right off her feet.

She wriggled in wincing fits and starts as he carried her through the room to the kitchen. "I'm not some sack of feed!" But he wasn't tossing her over his shoulder like she'd seen him do with countless burlap bags weighing almost as much as she. If anything, he was carrying her with inordinate care.

He pushed through the door and she ducked her forehead against his shoulder as the cold air whipped over them.

She held her breath as they went down the steps. "What are you going to do, take me out and toss me in a snowbank somewhere with nobody the wiser?"

"Yup." He pulled open the door of the truck, and it squealed loudly. "How did you guess?" He tucked her inside and fastened the safety belt around her, trapping her even more effectively.

She shook her head, freeing her chin and mouth from the folds of the quilt. "Seriously—"

He shut the door in her face, leaving her gaping like a trussed-up fish. Feeling that she'd already made a big enough fool of herself, she managed not to speak again until they were rattling their way back through the outskirts of town. "I *was* going to sleep back there, you know."

"Yeah, I could tell by the way you were staring into space." He slowed at an intersection for a moment, then went right on through.

"That was a red light," she pointed out.

"Did you see any oncoming traffic?" He turned a corner.

"That is beside the point."

"I remember when there wasn't a light at that corner." He gave her a look. "Back before people like you started coming around."

"I'm not to blame for the progress around Thunder Canyon." She was just there to capitalize on it. "That started up a few years ago thanks to a gold nugget some little kid found."

"He's not some kid. He's Erik Stevenson, and his stepmom, Faith, and I were in school together."

Had Russ and this Faith person dated? She managed to squelch the question in favor of one that should have been much more important. "*Where* are we going?"

"You ask a lot of questions."

She didn't mistake the comment for a compliment.

But as it turned out, the answer seemed perfectly obvious when he turned into a parking lot and drove around to the emergency room entrance of Thunder Canyon General Hospital.

She let out a huff. "You've got to be kidding me."

"Nope." He parked flagrantly in a vividly red curbed no-parking zone. He plucked her out of the seat again and carted her toward the sliding glass doors marking the entrance.

"Only you would ignore the half-dozen No Parking signs posted all around us. Are *they* a new addition to Thunder Canyon, too, because of dreaded people like me?"

"Be quiet."

"I don't appreciate being told to hush up like a naughty little girl."

He dumped her in the seat of an empty wheelchair sitting inside the entrance and braced his hands on the armrests on either side of her. "Keep up the lip," he murmured, leaning close to her face, "and before you can blink, gossip will get around this town that the latest newlyweds are already on the outs."

She flushed. Started to snap back that she could not possibly care less, only to rethink the matter just as quickly. "I'm not sick," she finally settled for. "I've never been in a hospital in my life."

"Born in a cab, were you?"

"Oh, funny. I told you earlier. I don't need a doctor, much less an emergency room." The idea of one made nervous needles join the assortment of pangs jangling inside of her.

"Humor me." His gaze dropped to her lips as if he were waiting for words to emerge. When they didn't, he nodded slightly, looking satisfied. "Wait here."

She couldn't very well do anything else, she thought, since she was still trapped in swaddling quilt. He strode over to the reception desk where—giving every impression of a doting, concerned husband—he told them that his bride needed X-rays.

Within minutes, a cheerful nurse was commandeering the handles on her wheelchair, steering her toward a wide, swinging door. "We'll have you fixed up in no time, Mrs. Chilton. Your husband can come on back with you, if you like."

"Thank you," she said huskily. "I *would* like."

She was out of her mind. Purely and simply.

Because the words were true.

Chapter Eleven

"I told you I didn't have any broken ribs," Melanie said three hours later when they were finally back at the Hopping H.

"So your self-diagnosis was lucky." He tucked two pillows behind her back and shoved the nail-studded leather ottoman more fully beneath her stockinged feet. "At least I'll sleep what's left of this night not thinking I might find you in the morning dead from a punctured lung."

"Then you'd have the entire Hopping H." She immediately regretted the waspish comment, even before he gave her a disgusted look and strode out of the room. He was back in seconds, though, bearing an old-fashioned-looking ice bag. "That was uncalled for. I'm sorry, Russ."

He leaned over her, yanked up her black top and pressed the very chilly ice bag against her bruised ribs. "Yup," he agreed. "You are sorry."

She yelped, but there was no space to back away from the cold.

He straightened, looking unsympathetic, despite the way he tossed the quilt over her legs. Not that she deserved any sympathy, acting like a spoiled brat the way she had.

"Thank you. For the ice…a-and everything." She held the ice bag more gingerly against her rib cage.

"It's as hard for you to express gratitude as it is to accept help," he commented as unemotionally as if he were observing a bug. "Why?"

She scrunched the hem of the soft quilt in her hands. "Maybe we should just agree that there are things I don't want to discuss and there are things that you don't want to discuss and leave it at that." She'd put her curiosity—her stupid little crush, or whatever fanciful imaginings where he was concerned—back in a box where it belonged, and he could do the same. "All right?"

"Right." His voice was dry as dust. "Since that's been working for us so well."

Her cheeks heated, but she lifted her chin. "Well, what would *you* suggest?"

He crouched down in front of the fire that had burned down to red embers while they were gone, and shoved the iron poker into the wood, causing a shower of sparks to fall from the charred remains. He grabbed another log from the stack on the hearth, tossed it onto the grate and jabbed the embers some more, creating yet another small explosion of red and gold fiery specks. "I don't know," he finally said, sounding weary. "Are you warm enough yet?"

"Aside from the ice bag freezing my ribs? Yes. Thank you."

"Frozen means numb. Consider that a blessing."

She moistened her lips. "You sound like you speak from experience."

"I've broken a few bones over the years. Do you need water or anything?"

She shook her head. She'd taken a dose of the mild painkiller they'd prescribed at the hospital before they'd left. "I'll be fine. If you're wanting to leave."

"I'm wanting a bunch of things," he murmured. But instead of heading for the coatrack where he'd dumped both of their coats when they arrived, he headed for the stairs, turning off the hanging wagon-wheel chandelier as he went. "Yell if you change your mind."

"I thought you were staying at the Flying J tonight."

"Yup." He didn't look back as he continued up the steps.

Melanie stared at the staircase even after he'd disappeared from sight. From overhead, she heard the faint sound of a door closing, and then the only thing she could hear was the sound of her pulse beating inside her head, accented by the snapping of the wood in the fireplace as the flame bit into its fresh fuel supply.

The wedding gifts were still on the end of the couch where he'd unloaded them earlier. At least a dozen boxes and gift bags festooned with ribbons and bows, some white, some silver, some ivory.

All lovely. And all sitting there, mocking her with their wedding-themed wrappings.

She shifted around on the couch until she was stretched out again. Her toes didn't even reach the stack of gifts. She knew she'd have to open them soon. Send the appropriate thank-you cards.

But the task seemed more than she could bear.

Sighing, she pulled the quilt up around her ears and, cradling the ice bag against her, she closed her eyes against the firelight and the gifts.

If only it were so easy to close her thoughts down, too.

But finally, the interminably long day and night had its way, and Melanie fell asleep, only to waken what seemed moments later when there was a loud pounding on the front door.

Groggy, she dragged herself off the couch and nearly tripped over the quilt tangling around her legs.

The room was bright with sunshine and the pounding on the door continued.

"I'm coming," she called out, pushing her hair out of her face and the quilt off her feet. She was nearly to the door before she realized she still had the ice bag— now warm and sloshy—tucked beneath her top and she yanked it out, dropping it on the stack of five-gallon paint drums sitting near the door. The door that was nearly rattling off its hinges—a considerable feat, given the size and weight of the enormous slab of wood.

"What's the emerg—" She dragged it open, only to go silent at the sight of her brother standing on the threshold. "Connor." She squinted into the bright sunlight, trying to see past him. What time was it? And had anyone *else* from the family accompanied him? "What are you doing here?"

Connor was five years her senior, and while she felt like something the cat had dragged in, he looked his very typical, urbane self, from his expensively cut auburn hair to the toes of his even more expensively made leather loafers.

Which were probably on the edge of ruin having had to trek through the slushy snow and gravel from the unfamiliar SUV parked behind Russ's ancient pickup truck.

"I was in the area," he said, looking down his long, thin nose at her.

She barely kept from snorting. Connor McFarlane loved cities. The larger the better. Period. "Thunder Canyon is a little small for your tastes, isn't it?"

"Are you going to invite me in or leave me standing out here on the step?"

The "step" was a forty-foot-wide stone porch that was a visual delight. But pointing that out to Connor would be pointless. She stepped back, pulling the door wide. "I guess you can come in." She tucked her tongue into her cheek. "Seeing as how you're in the area and all."

He entered, shrugging off his long, black wool coat and eyed the coatrack next to the door that was already hanging with Russ's sheepskin coat and the faded, stained jacket that he often wore while doing chores.

Connor folded his coat and looped it over his arm.

Melanie almost laughed. Which meant that, maybe, her time in Thunder Canyon had been productive in more ways than one.

She pushed the door closed. Russ's coats *were* on the coatrack, which meant that he couldn't be too far away.

She didn't want to examine too closely why that seemed a comforting thought.

Connor was busy looking around the large great room with its eclectic collection of furnishings and construction materials. "You're planning to be ready for guests in February?"

She folded her arms across her chest. Her muscles protested, but not as violently as they had the previous night. Maybe her painkiller hadn't quite worn off, yet. "That's right."

He shook his head. "It'll never happen."

"Just because *you* couldn't get the reno of your shop done on budget and on time doesn't mean I won't." She didn't have the luxury of unlimited McFarlane funds at her disposal, either.

"You'd compare *this*," Connor lifted one long-fingered hand to encompass their surroundings, "with a McFarlane House?"

Trust him to parry her thrust with his usual elitism. "This," she assured pointedly, "*is* a McFarlane house. Mine."

"And mine." Russ spoke behind her. A moment later, his hand closed over her shoulder.

It was all she could do not to jump out of her skin.

"I suppose you're my sister's latest folly."

"That's right. Russ Chilton." Russ extended his hand. "Nice to meet you," he drawled.

Looking reluctant, Connor shook his hand. "Connor McFarlane."

Russ grinned. Looked at his palm, then wiped it down his shirt. "I've been out with the cows," he said, sounding amused. "Was just gonna take your coat."

Melanie stifled a smile, silently wondering how badly her brother wanted to look at his own palm, to see what sort of crud he might have picked up. It seemed odd to think her brother might be even a bit unnerved. But he wasn't usually blatantly rude to strangers. And he ought to have picked up that Russ was merely playing to Connor's clearly obvious low expectations.

"I'm not staying long," Connor said.

"No kidding?" Russ shrugged. "Seems a long way to come to see your family and head on out again after just a few minutes. It's nearly lunchtime."

Melanie started. "It's that late?"

He looked amused as he shot Connor a look. "You know how it is with newlyweds."

She flushed.

Connor looked as if he had suddenly stepped in something as unappetizing as what he suspected might have been on Russ's hands. And as embarrassed as she felt, she was more annoyed with her brother for his mammoth-sized superiority complex. As far as he should be concerned, she was blissfully, newly married. He should be congratulating them both, not turning up his nose at her spouse.

"My brother and his wife, Jennifer, have been married so long he's probably forgotten," she told Russ.

Connor sighed. "If you could put aside the personal comments, we have some business to discuss."

"What else is family for but business?" Her smile was forced and she avoided the close look that Russ gave her. "Particularly ours."

Connor gave Russ a pointed look.

"Oh, Russ and I have no secrets," Melanie blithely lied. "Discuss away."

Looking displeased—a skill he'd learned well from their parents—he drew a folded packet of papers out of his lapel pocket. He extended them to her.

She didn't take them. "What is that?"

"Information from Donovan."

"About what?"

"About your current situation."

"There's nothing that he would have to say about what I'm doing these days that interests me."

"Don't be so sure."

"Fascinating as this all is," Russ inserted, "I've got chores waiting. I'm gonna grab a sandwich first. Want one?"

Melanie's stomach felt positively cavernous. "Maybe in a little while." She waited until Russ had left the room before looking back at her brother and lowered her voice. "What are you *really* doing here?"

"I told you. I was in the area."

She raised her brows. "To deliver those?" she gestured at the papers he still held. "That's what the postal service is usually for, isn't it?"

He tossed the pages onto the couch. "Maybe I wanted to get in some skiing, too."

"You've always preferred Gstaad. Why don't you just admit that you're here on a spying expedition for Mother and Dad?"

Connor's gaze drifted over the lamentably rough, in-progress state surrounding them. "If I were, imagine how pleased they're going to be with the report." His voice was ironic.

"Renovations are messy." She hated sounding defensive. She really hated that Russ was still within earshot, undoubtedly overhearing every word.

"Particularly messy when you're starting at an inferior level to begin with."

Her lips tightened. "Always good to know I have the support of my big brother. Oh, wait. That's right. Backstabbing is more your method."

"You're being ridiculous."

She was thoroughly sick of being told that. "How would you react if *your* management had been constantly second-guessed?"

"It's a moot point," Connor said smoothly. "My abilities are unquestioned."

"Bully for you," she muttered. The top of her head felt as if it were ready to blow right off. "And interestingly enough, considering how Mother's work has never been questioned, I can't even blame everyone's distrust of my abilities on sexism. Which means it is...just...me."

"And as usual, you're also overreacting."

"Incompetent and reactionary. That's me."

"I think you're highly competent."

Connor's head jerked as Russ reentered the room, a thick sandwich in one hand. "This doesn't concern you."

Seeming to give Connor's statement some consideration, Russ ambled farther into the room. "Since it's my wife you're insulting, I think maybe it does." He didn't stop until he stood next to Melanie and she knew there was no way he could miss the way she was trembling. Particularly when he slid his warm fingers through hers and lifted her cold hand, pressing his lips against the back of it. "Right, honey?"

"Nobody in our family is taking this—" Connor waved his hand dismissively "—marriage of yours seriously."

"The marriage license we signed is pretty serious," Melanie said.

"You just want attention."

Melanie swallowed down a fresh knot of anger.

"How long *have* you been married?" Russ asked, before she could summon an appropriately scathing retort.

Connor looked even more peeved. "What does that have to do with anything?"

"Just that I pity your wife," Russ said, still very much the good ol' boy. He swallowed a large bite of sandwich.

"Jennifer does not need the pity of some small-town, backwoods rancher."

"Maybe not," Russ returned evenly. "Maybe she's as uptight and asinine as you are, and you're perfectly suited for each other."

Connor's cold gaze fastened on Melanie's face. "Speak to your husband."

Melanie leaned against Russ's side. Whether it was all a lie or not, she felt stronger just from his being near. "Trust me, Connor. Russ and I do far more than speak to one another. You see, unlike all the men you and Mother and Donovan all seemed to think I should settle on, it turns out that small-town ranchers are my idea of a perfect mate."

Connor's throat looked oddly florid above his beautifully knotted silk tie.

"Maybe you and Jen really have forgotten how to behave like normal married people," she continued, feeling a genuine spurt of pity. "Or maybe you never learned, considering the example our parents set. But fortunately, that is not *our* situation."

Russ squeezed her hand. She didn't know whether to interpret it as encouragement or warning. Encouragement seemed odd, but then so did his entirely supportive stance.

The man possessed acting skills she'd never expected.

"I don't suppose you showed some good sense to have even a minimally suitable prenup."

"Whatever for? What's mine is his."

Her brother looked nearly apoplectic.

"She's just teasing you," Russ said. His voice was still cold, but there was an unholy laughter in his eyes. "We have an agreement. We both agreed it was necessary."

"Thank heavens for some small mercies." Connor eyed them both. "When you've come to your senses, there's still a place for you back home," he told her.

"Isn't it polite to wait at least a few months before predicting doom for a marriage?"

"He's not talking about our marriage," Melanie told Russ. "Isn't that right, Connor?"

Her brother shook out his coat, sending the clear signal that, as far as he was concerned, conversation was finished. "The annual McFarlane Christmas event is in little more than a week."

"I'm not likely to forget." The enormous celebration had been held every year on Christmas Eve for as long as she could remember.

He pulled on his coat. "I'll have my secretary arrange your travel."

Her teeth set on edge, all over again. "I'm more than capable of making my own arrangements, Connor."

"She'll be in touch with you soon." He bussed her cheek, ignored Russ completely and strode right out of the door without a backward glance.

Melanie let out a breath into the long silence that followed his exit. "Well. That, um, that was my brother."

"Pleasant guy." Russ finished his sandwich in one bite and picked up the folded papers that Connor had left on the couch. He held them out to her. "Seems like the kind of person who'd run a background check on a family interloper."

"That's not a dossier about you," she said with certainty. "Go ahead. Look." She knew it would open a passel of questions, but suddenly it just didn't seem to matter. He'd already overheard plenty, anyway.

He flipped open the folds. Frowned a little. "This is an offer to purchase the Hopping H. For—" he kept reading, then pursed his lips in a silent whistle "—a helluva lot of money." He glanced at her. "What's the deal, Red? I thought McFarlane money was backing this little project?"

"No."

His eyes narrowed. "So there's not going to be a granite sign on the main gate welcoming people to McFarlane House Thunder Canyon?"

She lifted her chin. She knew that was the impression that most people had. An impression that she'd done nothing to correct. "The sign will continue to say

Hopping H with the addition of Guest Ranch beneath it. Is that a problem?"

"It's your own money on this," he pressed. "Are you financed by anyone?"

"No."

"You're doing this completely on your own?"

"I'm trying," she said more defensively than she liked.

He tossed the papers back on the couch and propped his hands on his hips, eyeing her. "*Why* didn't you just say so before? Don't tell me that this whole guest ranch thing is some lifelong dream of yours, because that dog won't run."

"My lifelong dream was to do exactly what I was raised to do. Run a McFarlane House."

"But you're not. What happened? Did you quit? Get fired?"

Words clambered up her chest, but were held back by the dam in her tight throat. "My family would never have fired me."

"So you quit." He made it sound like a mortal sin.

"People do that, sometimes."

He looked around the great room. "Not you."

His calm observation helped center her. She moistened her lips. "I need them to realize I can succeed on my own without their interference or influence."

"And then what?"

She opened her mouth, but no answer came.

Russ finally let out a breath. "Well. Judging by your brother's open-armed welcome of me, I'm sort of curious why you thought it was important that your family think we're married. Unless you just wanted to rub an unsuitable match in their face."

"There's nothing unsuitable about you. And Connor's attitude had nothing to do with our marriage, anyway."

He smiled sardonically. "Didn't sound that way to me."

"You're worth ten Connors. Believe me. He doesn't stoop to help anyone unless he profits from it or it makes him look good."

He picked up her hand, touching the wedding band still on her finger. "And how, exactly, does that make me different?"

She pulled away. Of course she couldn't afford to forget that Russ was only in this agreement for his own benefit. He wanted to protect his future interest in the Hopping H. They'd been married—oh, it seemed odd to even think that—for only two weeks. She needed to do a better job of remembering just exactly *why* they were married.

She picked up the thawed ice bag. She supposed he'd watched out for her the night before because it was expedient. "I guess it doesn't," she said, heading out of the room. "I guess we're all very much the same."

The thought seemed unbearably sad.

Chapter Twelve

"What are you working on?"

Melanie looked up from the blueprints she'd been studying when Russ walked into the room later that week.

Since Connor's visit, Russ had spent most of his time away from the ranch house. During the day. During the night.

She knew she should have pushed him on the issue—he was supposed to be teaching her the ranching ropes—but like the coward she was, she kept putting it off, focusing her energies instead on the other matters that had been neglected since their elopement.

Now, her foolish nerves jangled at his unexpected appearance, and her greedy eyes took him in despite her stern, mental reminder, not to forget either one of their motives. "The layout of the creek-side cabins." Her voice was husky and she coughed a little.

"You getting sick?"

She flushed. Not physically. Emotionally? She felt as though she were withering.

She rested her elbows on the top of the desk. "No. I just, um, just swallowed wrong."

What had prompted his appearance? It was the middle of the morning. Too late for breakfast. Too early for lunch. Not that he'd eaten either one of those meals with her lately. Not that she should care. Sharing meals hadn't been specifically stipulated in that agreement of theirs.

"What's all that stuff?" He nodded toward the cardboard boxes stacked next to the front door.

"I unwrapped the wedding gifts." And what a depressing task that had been, doing it alone. "I sent out the thank-you cards yesterday. I, um, I signed your name, too."

He grunted a little. Flipped open the top carton. "Why are they in the boxes?"

"So it'll be easy to keep them organized. For returning. Donating. Whatever." Keeping the gifts, given the situation, seemed out of the question. "How are things at the Flying J?" As a fishing expedition, it was pretty weak. But, darn it, she didn't want to think anymore about the gifts, and she *was* interested in how, and where, he'd been spending his time. No amount of lying to herself convinced her that interest wasn't expressly personal.

"Same as ever." He shrugged out of his coat and tossed it on the coatrack, only to stop short at the sight of the finished media room. "Holy sh—oot. Think you got a big enough television there, princess?" He headed toward the area off the great room and beneath his booted footsteps, the nearly completed planked floor sounded wonderfully solid. He stopped next to the flat-screen television that was mounted directly on the wall. "Ever heard of overkill? A person could watch this from the next county."

"When you're watching the Super Bowl on it, I imagine you'll think differently." The zenith of football games was still many weeks away, though she hoped to be open for guests by then. Would Russ be even more absent by then?

He made a considering sound. "Maybe."

Which told her nothing at all.

She stifled a sigh and schooled her features when he turned back toward her. He ran his hand along the back of the leather chairs that were situated in semicircular rows, facing the television as he headed toward her. "Guess you've had a busy few days."

"Yes." She slid the cap on her pen and held one end in each hand, slowly rolling it between her fingers. She stopped, though, when his gaze seemed to go to her fidgeting fingers. Did he notice that she was still wearing the wedding ring?

She hadn't removed it since the party at the Gallatin Room and now she wished she had. It seemed glaringly obvious there on her hand below the long cuff of her black sweater.

"Sort of expected to see a Christmas tree up over here or something by now."

She lifted her shoulder. "What for?" It wasn't as if they were going to be spending the holiday together, like a cozy, normal newlywed couple.

If anything, the thought of putting up a tree—given their situation—was pretty depressing.

"My construction crew has been here every day," she added rapidly, hoping he'd drop the topic. "They brought in a third man, too. You just missed them, actually. They've been working in the bathrooms upstairs today and ran into town to replace some parts that were wrong."

"Does that mean we don't have to share anymore?"

She dropped the pen onto the blueprints. Sitting back in her chair, she folded her hands together in her lap where he couldn't see them. "No more sharing. Is that why you haven't been here, lately? Because of the shortage of operable bathrooms?"

He snorted softly. "Right. You know me, babe." His teeth flashed in an ironic smile. "I like my own primping space."

She managed a roll of her eyes and felt her nerves crank another notch tighter when he came up next to the desk and leaned over her and the blueprints, bracing one arm to the side.

He smelled like fresh air, winter and mint all rolled into one and if she moved three inches, she could have rested her head on the soft navy flannel shirt stretched across his shoulders.

"So?"

She started. "So, what?"

"What are you checking over with the prints, here?"

"Just some dimensions for the interior designer."

"Pity. Thought you were considering moving the cabins altogether, along with the fishing dock, the way I suggested."

She stared at the plans. Better the oversize, scaled drawing than at that hard jaw just inches from her head. "It's better where I've already planned."

"What'd I tell you about the fishing?"

She smiled tightly. "If I move the dock where you suggested, it'll be located within the area *you* want when the land is split up." She knew, because she'd checked.

"So?"

"So, what are you going to want, Russ? For me to lease back the acreage from you?" She shook her head, laughing a little and rolled the plans back into a tube, snapping a rubber band around them to hold them in place. "I don't think so. The dock stays where it's planned."

He exhaled. "Good grief. Come on." He grabbed her beneath her arm and practically lifted her out of her chair.

She squeaked with surprise and the blueprints rolled off the desk onto the chair that she'd graduated to from the wooden crate. "What?"

He pulled her across the room, skirting the paint gallons that seemed to be multiplying on their own. "You want your guests to have the ultimate experience, but *you* haven't even seen it for yourself. Consider this more of your ranching education."

She set her boot heels, as much against his unexpected suggestion as the surge of something seductively bright and light inside her that was owed entirely, dangerously, to him. "What do you want to do? Go fishing in the dead of winter?"

"Creek's still flowing."

"But it's cold out there!"

"That's what coats and gloves are for." He grabbed the smaller-sized parka off the rack. "And it's unseasonably warm out there, anyway, in case you haven't noticed. But I am glad to see you found something more suitable than that fur coat of yours."

"I only wear that for dressy occasions," she defended, only to realize too late that he was deliberately goading her.

She snatched the parka from him and slid into it, pulling up the zipper with a decisive rasp.

He shrugged into his sheepskin coat. "Gloves?"

She reached into her pockets and pulled out a sturdy pair, holding them up triumphantly.

"Mmm. Good. Not as interesting as panties," he murmured and pulled open the heavy front door. "But good."

She flushed to the roots of her hair. "You *could* just forget about that, you know."

"I could," he agreed. "But—"

"I know," she cut him off. "Where would be the fun in that?"

"Exactly."

She followed him down the wide steps only to stop short at the sight of yet another ancient-looking pickup truck, this one a vile shade of orange. "What happened to the other truck?"

"Nothing. I pulled the engine yesterday. Still have some work to do on it." He pulled open the passenger door.

Melanie blinked a little, but moved past him and climbed up into the truck. It seemed impossible, but she suspected it was even older than the last one. The faded upholstery on the long bench seat was tattered and fraying, but when she ran her hand across it, she couldn't feel any springs poking through. "Don't we need fishing gear or something?" she asked him when he got behind the wheel.

"We'll run by the J and grab some."

It seemed awfully out of the way in his attempt to convince her to move the dock and the cabins farther north, but she couldn't bring herself to protest.

And wasn't that a fine kettle of fish?

The man kept himself scarce for a few days, and she was ready to agree to just about anything for a few minutes of his company.

She watched him from the corner of her eye as he wheeled the truck around and headed for the hill leading down to the main gate. "Joey's been a big help these past few days." The young man had been a regular presence around the Hopping H, doing all of the things that Russ had been previously taking care of.

Before he'd seen firsthand what kind of family she came from.

"Joey's a good kid," he said.

The truck bounced along for a while.

She toyed with the gloves she still held in her hand and searched for something to say. "Do you have any special plans for Christmas?"

He slanted a glance toward her, then looked back at the road, evidently satisfied that she wasn't probing into too personal a territory. "Steph and Grant's wedding is on Christmas Day."

"Right. Of course. She mentioned that the other night. You're Grant's best man?"

"Yeah. Not much to do, though. Claims he doesn't want a bachelor party." He grinned faintly. "Says we've partied often enough in the past to make up for it."

She could just imagine the two men together. Both impossibly attractive in their own ways. The women they'd set their eyes on had probably been doomed from the starting gate. "Is it a large wedding?"

"Don't know. Didn't ask. All I know is I've gotta wear some fool penguin suit." He grimaced at the very idea of it.

She hid a smile. "That I would have liked to have seen." The words were true. Not because he'd be so uncomfortable in formal wear as his expression suggested, but because she knew he'd look spectacular.

On second thought, she was probably better off missing the event. She was finding it difficult enough to keep the man pegged in his appropriate slot.

"Why wouldn't you?" He glanced at her again. "You're not really going back to Philadelphia for that Christmas thing your brother was yammering about, are you?"

She folded her hand around the gloves and looked away from him. "They're expecting me."

"To toe the line."

"It's an annual event. We don't just invite employees. There are dignitaries, celebrities, relatives."

"Interesting how you put the family members last." He turned off the highway again, driving past the iron Flying J brand that swung from the opened gate. "What relatives besides your brother and parents?"

"A few distant cousins. A great-aunt." She nibbled at her lip. "I've never missed a McFarlane Christmas party." She'd never before contemplated it. Not even when her anger and hurt over her father's duplicity had been at its peak.

"Worried you'll be disinherited if you're a no-show?"

"No. I used to enjoy the party."

"Used to." He pulled up behind the house in the same place he had the morning they'd gone to Las Vegas. "When'd you stop?"

She frowned a little. "I...I haven't stopped enjoying the party." Had she? She tucked her fingers into her gloves. With the truck stopped, the cold was quickly noticeable.

"Yeah, the expression on your face tells me you can't *wait* to get there." His voice was dry. "You gonna sit out here or wait inside while I grab up some fishing tackle and rods?"

She looked up at the house. *His* house. "I-inside." She pushed open the door and followed him up the back steps.

He held open the storm door for her and when she was inside, just gestured vaguely. "I'll be a few minutes." He stomped through the mudroom into the adjoining kitchen, and then disappeared up the narrow staircase that led right off the kitchen.

Melanie eyed the washing machine and dryer sitting next to each other at one end of the rectangular mudroom. In comparison to the high-tech models she'd had to learn how to operate, his appliances looked like something out of a 1960's advertisement. The kitchen was also stuck in the same time warp. The wood planks of the floor were clean but scraped and nicked from years of wear. The pine cabinets were flat-paneled and plain. The white refrigerator was no taller than she was and when she dared to pull on the long, chrome handle to open it, she saw that it had one of those old-fashioned freezers inside at the top that was barely large enough to hold an ice tray.

Knowing she was snooping didn't stop her from glancing down the contents of the narrow shelves. Milk. Beer. A loaf of bread and a bag of apples.

At the sound of a footfall overhead, she quickly closed the refrigerator door and pulled out one of the kitchen chairs from the square Formica-topped table pushed beneath the lone window. Looking out, she oriented herself and realized the view Russ had from this spot was of Hopping H land.

She was still sitting there, looking out, when Russ returned with a big tool-box-looking thing that he dumped on the table. "Hold these." He handed her two fishing rods.

"You're serious about us fishing."

"Evidently."

She tucked her tongue behind her teeth for a moment. "I've never fished in my life," she finally admitted.

"Shocking." His bland voice didn't mask his amusement. "I'll call the local paper."

She made a face. "I'm perfectly willing to go see this prime area you're so set on, but if you're determined to put this thing—" she jiggled the fishing rods "—in the water, I'll just watch. If you don't mind."

"I do. And the only thing that goes in the water is the hook, line and this." He pulled a squat plastic container from where he'd tucked it under his arm, and set it on the table.

"Soft-spread margarine?"

He flipped the plastic lid off the container.

She grimaced at the sight of the slowly writhing brown mass of goo inside it and sat back in her chair, well away from it. "Yuck."

"It's just worms and dirt, princess."

Which probably explained the holes that were punched in the plastic lid. "I'll take your word for it."

He scooped his finger into the container and lifted out a long, writhing beastie. "See?"

If she leaned back any farther in her seat, she was going to tip it over. "Lovely. I'll *definitely* just watch."

He chuckled and dropped the worm back into the container, then fit the lid back on top. He shoved his hand beneath the water faucet. "If you've gotta pee, do it now. Only thing out by the creek are winter bare trees and snowbanks. Doesn't bother me, but you might not like such facilities." He jerked his chin toward the staircase. "Only one bathroom. Top of the stairs."

She flushed, but nevertheless headed for the stairs.

The bathroom was just as ancient in its design as the kitchen and she couldn't help but imagine Russ maneuvering his tall body and wide shoulders within the confines of the small shower stall. When she was finished, she resolutely corralled her curiosity to explore further and returned to the kitchen.

She could see Russ was already outside behind the wheel, and she grimaced at the sight of the worm container still sitting on the table. He hadn't left it there unintentionally.

She was loath to touch it, but if he thought she was going to go out there and give him even more reason to consider her a spoiled princess, he had another thing coming.

She snatched the dish towel with its odd crocheted loop on one end from the knob on the front of the stove where it was hanging, and wrapped it around the container before carrying it out to the truck.

He didn't bother holding back a derisive laugh when he saw what she'd done. "You're using one of my mother's favorite dish towels to carry those worms, you know."

She set the container on the seat between them, more to his side than hers. "My apologies to your mother's memory," she said, not insincerely. She couldn't quite tell if he was pulling her leg about the towel or not. But the fact that it had been his mother's and that it was still in use in his kitchen to this day struck her as quite… touching. And she really didn't want to be touched by anything that concerned him.

She already feared that he would be her downfall.

He just shook his head again, thankfully unaware of her tangled thoughts. Humor was still in his expression. "Don't sweat it. She probably wiped my butt when I was a baby with that towel a time or two, as well."

Her cheeks hot, she looked out the side window. "Is it supposed to snow?"

"Not the most subtle way of changing the topic," he observed. "But the forecast wasn't calling for it. It's too warm." He leaned over the steering wheel, looking up through the windshield as he drove away from the house. "Clouds are looking like it, though. I'll check your wood supply before tonight, just to be safe."

Getting that assurance from him hadn't been her intention at all. But still, the consideration from him was welcomed, if somewhat unexpected. "Thank you." She watched the landscape as they drove back toward the gate. "I didn't realize you could see the Hopping H from your place."

"We border each other."

As if she could forget. "I know. I just didn't know that your house was so close to that border."

He shrugged.

She nibbled the inside of her lip for another moment and tried not to imagine the worms squirming around inside that container. "Those holes in the lid are too small for a worm to get through, right?"

He gave her a deadpan look. "Yeah. Sure."

She shuddered.

He laughed.

Despite herself, she couldn't keep her lips from twitching. So she looked out the side window to hide it from him. "The Hopping H's house is quite a bit larger than yours."

"It's about half a century newer, too. My great-grandfather homesteaded on the J. My grandfather built the house himself. My dad was born in it."

Fascinated despite her intentions otherwise, she turned back to him. "Right there in the house?"

"Yeah. We didn't always have a hospital here in Thunder Canyon," he reminded her dryly. "Though it did come well before we had our recent gold rush." He pulled onto the soft shoulder and pointed out her window where they could see the edges of the town. "That used to be nothing but open land," he told her. "Now it's a flippin' condominium project. One of those master planned communities." He shook his head, obviously disgusted with the very notion of it. "Time was when a kid could go riding on his bike from anywhere in town all the way across it and never encounter a stranger. Now?" He shook his head again. "Now we've got a damned dinner theater with the Thunder Canyon Cowboys shaking their butts in front of tables full of people who think that's what a real cowboy does."

"I think the people who watch the Thunder Canyon Cowboys know the difference," Melanie said mildly. "Have you even seen the show?"

"Hell, no."

"Then don't be so quick to judge. It's pretty entertaining, in fact. What's so bad about that?"

"It's all changing. And not for the better. If you knew the Thunder Canyon *I* know, you'd see that."

"Which brings us right back to the reason you resent my presence here. The Thunder Canyon you want has given way to progress, and I'm one more representative of that."

"I don't—" He broke off and let out a long sigh. "I don't resent you."

Her throat was tight. "You don't like me much, though."

"I wish I liked you less," he said flatly. "My life would be a lot easier. And don't sit there giving me that wide-eyed, startled look," he added when she just stared at him. "You know I want you. Why the hell do you think I've been staying away from you lately?"

She swallowed hard. If she could have conjured a smart reply, she would have. But nothing hung in her mind except the cold, bare truth. "I thought it had to do with Connor."

"Your brother's a jerk, honey, but he's not the one I promised not to hanky or panky with." His brooding gaze burned down her face, making her cheeks even hotter. "You blush easier than anyone I've ever met. Must've been hell when you were a teenager and discovering boys."

Her "discovering" was severely limited, but she still would have choked before admitting it to anyone. Particularly Russ. "Are we, um, going to walk to the creek from here, or what?"

"Rather go fishing than talk about our sex-free marriage?" He put the truck in gear and drove back onto the empty road. "Seems like that should put things into perspective for a man."

"Does it?" She flattened her palms on her thighs. "If you feel the, um, the way you do, then what are we doing out here now? I mean, why go to the trouble with the fishing equipment and those?" She tilted her head toward the worms. "Why bother with anything that's not in our agreement?" His face looked set in stone and she sighed heavily. "Just take me back to the Hopping H."

"You need to see the creek for yourself. See what Thunder Canyon—*my* Thunder Canyon—still offers."

"I'll hire an expert who can study the creek and the most advantageous positioning for the guest cabins."

He practically stood on the brakes again, pulling off the road once more. "Damn, woman. What is it with you and *hiring* people?"

"I don't mean any offense to you," she said quickly. "I'm sure you're well versed with the best fishing, but there are other considerations—"

"Screw being offended," he cut her off. "This isn't about me. It's about you. Is it not in your DNA to listen to suggestions or advice unless you've forked over some dough for it first?"

She winced. "I'm not supposed to need help, okay?"

He stared at her as if she'd grown a second head. "*Everyone* needs help, Melanie."

"Not a McFarlane."

"If your brother is anything to go by, I'd say y'all have built up a pretty hefty need for just that. Putting up money for everything probably helps you maintain that sense of superiority."

"Don't be ridiculous."

"Gotta keep the power and control on your side," he rolled right on. "Easier to accomplish that if you've paid for the privilege. Look at us. Hitched for profit on my part and power on yours."

"It is not about power. It is about not being weak!" She looked away from him, but the admission was already out there. She tried to draw in a breath, but it only sounded shaky. Which seemed fitting, since she was pretty much shaking from head to toe. And she couldn't blame it on the temperature, because the air spewing out the ancient vents of the pickup truck was thick and warm.

"Melanie, I told you before, I don't think you're weak."

She closed her eyes. "Don't go getting soft on me, now, Chilton. I don't need it."

"I wish I were soft," he muttered, and with a deft motion, flicked open her safety belt. "Things wouldn't be so damned difficult."

"What—" She broke off when he grabbed her by the waist and slid her bodily across the seat and right onto his lap.

She barely noticed the container of worms tumbling harmlessly to the floor of the truck.

His fingertips pressed into her waist, holding her tightly. "Do you get it now?" His voice was low. Rough. And it rasped, tantalizing, over her starved senses.

She stared at his lips, barely two inches away from her. Perfectly formed lips that didn't look too thin at all. Just painfully still. Unlike the muscle that flexed in his jaw.

She opened her mouth to speak, but the only thing that emerged was one, husky word. And right then, she couldn't bring herself to care that every needful yearning inside her seemed to shout out from it. *"Russ."*

He made a sound, deep in his throat. And still he didn't move. As if he'd done as much moving as he was going to do, dragging her onto his lap, where she could feel every hard inch of him. The tension in his wide shoulders, despite the thick coat. The hard muscle in his thighs, despite the thick denim. And all the region in between.

Her heart pounded inside her chest, dizzying.

Or perhaps it was just him that was dizzying.

She swallowed and closed her mind to common sense and all the sensible reasons why she should be scrambling back to her own side of the truck, and tilted her head, softly fitting her mouth to his.

Chapter Thirteen

She felt like a bird in his lap. A hungry bird, nipping at his lips, fingertips flexing against his cheek. His neck.

It was all Russ could do not to devour her.

He caught her head in his hands, holding her still. Pressed his forehead against hers and drew in a harsh, teeth-clenched breath. "Wait," he breathed out again. "Wait a sec."

They were on the side of the road where anybody and everybody could drive on past. Okay, so the Flying J and the Hopping H were about the only two spreads located out this way, but he could just imagine what a laugh they'd cause if word got around town that the latest newlyweds in Thunder Canyon couldn't keep their hands off each other long enough to get from one of their roofs to underneath the other.

"I'm sorry," she said. "I shouldn't have done that."

He managed to clear the gut-wrenching need fogging his vision for long enough to see the misery on her face. "Why? You promised to someone else?"

It didn't seem possible, but her expression grew even more wretched, her color even higher.

A stone settled in the pit of his stomach. "If you are, it's a helluva time to find out now. Why couldn't you go off and marry *him?*"

She was shaking her head. "No. No. There is no him. There's never—oh, God. Just bury me now." She ducked her forehead against his shoulder. "I thought you wanted this." Her voice was muffled.

He considered banging his head against the window. Maybe it would jar his brains back into some working order. Or at least clang 'em around until he could fathom the depths of this woman's mind. "It should seem pretty obvious what I want," he said pointedly.

"You said to stop."

He gave a bark of laughter, though he felt like laughing about as much as he felt like sticking his finger in a light socket. Because every breath, every word, every motion against her was a torment.

And he was a masochist, because he ran his hand down the back of her swaddling parka and searched beneath it until he found his way to those narrow, jean-clad hips. Hips that he circled in his hands and dragged a mind-blowing inch closer. "I said to *wait.*"

She was looking at him again. Those impossibly thick lashes looking soft and vulnerable around her wide, chocolate-brown eyes. "Why?"

"Why?" He swallowed a disbelieving oath. "Because if we didn't stop—didn't give me a second to remember that we're in a freaking truck—and I don't know about you, babe, but I'm too old for making it in a truck—there wasn't, *isn't,* going to be any stopping. Period."

Contrary woman that she was, instead of expressing some gratitude for what he considered pretty decent— he couldn't quite manage to think he'd found some gentlemanly tendencies at this stage—behavior, she was looking decidedly…intrigued.

And she'd somehow managed to unfasten his coat between them, slipping her slender, wicked fingers underneath.

They felt like hot pokers gliding over his chest.

God help him if she made it beneath his layer of flannel and T-shirt.

"If we don't stop, it'll be you…me…horizontal. Vertical. Truck or not. Doesn't much matter as long as it involves the two of us. Together." For an intelligent woman, she was aggravatingly slow on the uptake. "Get it?"

She tilted her head again, brushing her lips over the point of his chin, then gradually working her way upward—settling even more dangerously against him—toward his right ear. She slid one hand behind his neck, holding him prisoner with that light touch. "I'd like to get it." Her words were little more than a whisper against him.

A whisper that shot right down through him.

His hands clutched her hips. Roved over her thigh. Her rear. "Mel—*dammit,* woman!" He dumped her unceremoniously off his lap and raked his fingers through his hair, pressing his fingertips against his skull, which seemed almost ready to blow right off the top.

She half lay, half sat there. Sprawled, really—one knee bent, foot on the seat and her other on the floorboard—watching him silently.

Her coat was unzipped, that thin black sweater of hers clinging to her breasts. And *they* were moving with every deep, fast breath she took in. Her hair lay tousled around her jaw, enticingly dark flames compared to her smooth, ivory skin.

But what really got to him was the expression in her eyes. Always her eyes.

Naked need.

The same kind of need that had kept him awake for the past three nights. The same kind that had driven him back to the Hopping H, just to see her and shovel out some damn horse manure if that's what it took to get near enough to her—but not *too* near—without losing his mind.

He wrapped his hands around the hard, cold steering wheel. "We are *going* fishing."

For a long while, she met his statement with silence. Then her parka rustled when she finally pushed herself upright on her side of the seat. "Fine." She sounded subdued.

He leaned forward and knocked his forehead on the steering wheel. "The worst word in the English language between a man and a woman is *fine*," he muttered. It never boded well when a woman said *fine* to a man.

Never.

"Excuse me?"

Great. Back to Melanie the ultrapolite.

He straightened. Glared at her. "We're about halfway between your place and mine. Which will it be? Your bed is bigger than mine, so you just might want to keep that in mind."

The pink bloomed all over her face, all at once. Her cheeks. Her throat.

Even her lips looked pinker.

Oh, yeah. Pinker.

Softer.

Fuller.

His hands strangled the steering wheel even tighter. He was going to burn that infernal prenuptial napkin the first chance he got. One match to the soft, wrinkled white paper and *whoosh*.

It'd all be over.

Reason crept into his mind.

It *would* be all over. Except the two of them were married. For profit or power, for better or worse.

At least for the better part of five and a half more months.

He unhinged his fingers from the steering wheel. On the road, a truck with an enormous doug fir strapped in the truck bed was approaching. It slowed a little as it came abreast with them.

Russ lifted his hand in an absent wave and the other vehicle thankfully returned to speed and continued onward.

"We're going to have to do something about this hanky-panky rule of ours."

"I was trying," she said to the window beside her.

He let out a jagged sigh. "Saying things like that is not helping me any here."

"I'm a McFarlane. Isn't it more likely that I was only trying to help myself?"

He eyed her. Sitting so properly on her end of the seat—about as far as she could get away from him without pushing out the window—with her feet crossed at the ankle. As if she were wearing time-for-high-tea heels instead of corrugated-soled leather boots. She even had her hands folded together in her lap.

The cheap wedding ring was on her finger, still.

"Melanie, if we start sleeping together it's going to make things even stickier when it ends."

"And it *will* end."

Was she reaffirming that, or questioning it?

He blamed the debate on his infernally aroused imagination.

Of course their marriage would end. That's what marriages did. Particularly when they started out on such a promising note as theirs had.

He'd been head over heels for Nola, and that sure in hell had ended. Now he just sent monthly checks for the son who called another man dad.

"So let's just go fishing," he finally said. "Then when you have a guest wanting to know the best place to drop a hook and line, you'll be able to tell him or her based on your *own* experience, not from what you've learned from anyone else. Me, or some other Joe who'd be happy to take your money from you."

"Wouldn't you be happier if I couldn't fulfill the interests and wishes of my guests? If the guest ranch fails, then I'll be forced to sell. You could own the entire ranch, after all, for even less than your original offer was on the place."

Forget the ranch.

He almost said it. But good sense and self-control kept the words buried down inside where they belonged. "Or you could take up the offer your father made on the property."

"I'd give it away before I'd let him take it over, even if I did make some profit as a result."

He frowned. "Look at me."

Her parka rustled again. She finally angled her chin toward him, though her gaze wouldn't meet his. He tucked his knuckle beneath that stubborn chin and lifted.

Her lashes finally lifted and her eyes met his.

"Why would you say that?"

"Because it's true. I don't need rescuing by my father or anyone else in my family. They don't want the Hopping H for themselves. They just want to continue believing that I'm incapable of managing anything on my own."

"Maybe they want to *help*," he suggested.

Her lips lifted in a weary smile. "That's a four-letter word to the McFarlanes, remember? They don't want to help. They want to rule. Period." She leaned forward suddenly and gave him a long, speculative look when he actually jerked a little.

As if he were afraid she'd jump his bones?

More like, he knew his resistance to her was shot if she made one more encouraging movement toward him.

But she was merely reaching for the worm container that had rolled on the floor beneath his legs.

With ginger fingers, she set it on the seat beside them and then wiped her fingertips down the leg of her jeans.

He rolled down the window, letting in a welcome shot of cold air. "Why do you believe that?"

She exhaled. Shook her head.

Damn. She gave stubborn new meaning.

"If you answer my question, then I'll answer one of yours." He could already guess what it'd be about.

His son.

She lifted an eyebrow. "Sounds like a weird version of *I'll show you mine if you show me yours*."

"Played that with The Third, did you?"

"Who?"

"The kid in the hotel. The chef's kid."

"Ah. Mason." She shook her head, her expression finally lightening up. "Not exactly. He did kiss me on my cheek once, though. I thought I'd died and gone to heaven."

"There are better spots to kiss." Though her cheek was a good starting point. Soft. Smooth. Warm with the blood that ran through it, turning it pink. He mentally shook himself. "Sorry."

She moistened her lips. "Let's just go do this fishing thing of yours."

Stay and argue? Or get out of the too-tight confines of the truck where the only thing he seemed to be able to breathe in was the enticing scent of her?

He shoved the truck back into gear and spun the tires getting off the shoulder.

In order to get to the creek, he eventually had to turn off the road, and they cut across a fair portion of open land. Fortunately, the layer of snow was thin and crisp from age and the old truck capably handled the job.

"Are we on Hopping H land?"

"Flying J."

She made a soft *mmm.* "It's pretty here."

It was. The shelter belt of pine trees was still green and barely dusted with snow. Beyond that long, curving line of trees lay the bank of the creek, and as they bounced over the land, crossing from his property to hers via a scraggly piece of barbed wire that easily came off the fence post because he'd done it so often in the past, they could see the occasional glitter of flowing water.

When they passed the site for the cabins that she was thinking of, he stopped. "Here's your original site." No ground was broken yet. There weren't even any markers.

"How can *you* tell?"

"Because I know the Hopping H. I grew up here, remember? If I wasn't tramping around on my folks' property, I was tramping around over here. With permission, of course. There's not a boulder or tree here that I don't know."

She caught her lip between her teeth for a moment, studying him. Then she looked out the window, giving him no indication of her thoughts.

Amazing how she could do that, when sometimes everything she seemed to feel was written right on her face.

"I'm told that the creek is at its widest here," she said.

"It is. It makes good swimming, but that's about it."

"In a creek? With the creek…things…swimming around you, too?" She shuddered a little. "Give me good old chlorinated pools."

He chuckled. "Darlin', you don't know what you're missing. Only thing better than dipping in the creek on a hot afternoon is skinny-dipping in the creek on a hot afternoon."

Her lips firmed. "I suppose you've done plenty of *that.*"

Not in a few years. "Last time I went swimming— and no, we weren't nekkid—" he drawled out the word just to see if her cheeks colored, and they did "—was with my son."

She shot him a surprised look. And no wonder, since he was the one to have made that particular topic verboten.

He looked at the crystal-clear swirl of water. "He was seven." Why he told her that, he couldn't fathom.

"And he's ten now?"

"Yeah." His voice was more gruff than curt, and he shoved the truck into gear, pulling away from the area, and the memories. And either she'd learned her lesson well where off-limit topics were concerned, or she could see that he didn't want to dwell on the matter, because for once she didn't poke and probe.

Finally, they reached a small bend, and he pulled to a stop at the head of the creek bank just on the other side of it. To the south and the west, well out of their line of sight, lay the Hopping H buildings. "This is it." He pushed out of the truck.

She climbed out, too, zipping up her parka and stepping a little away from the truck. She was obviously studying the terrain, taking in the lay of the land.

He gathered up the gear from the truck bed. "Bring the worms when you're ready," he told her as he headed down the slight incline toward the water's edge.

She took her sweet time about it, which was probably a good thing. Gave him a chance to haul in the brisk air. Freeze the insides of his lungs a bit. Chill out everything else about him that had been set onto boil for a week or two too long.

He had a line in the water by the time she joined him, silently handing over the container, which she held, wrapped once more in his mother's dish towel. "Thought you needed bait," she said, looking at the fishing line bobbing with the creek's brisk current.

"I put on a lure while you were dawdling."

"Sure. *Now* you admit there was an alternative to the worms." She eyed the second tripod stool that he'd set up for her use. "You're not doing the whole fly-fishing thing?"

He shook his head. "Not today. Lazy man's fishing is what this is."

"I've never seen a chair that looks like that, before."

"Just enough to prop your butt on." He didn't dare glance at that particular object of hers, or he'd be right back in the same fix he'd started with.

Wanting his in-name-only wife more than he could stand.

She moved around the canvas-topped tripod and carefully lowered herself on it, only to nearly fall back on her butt.

He reached out and planted his hand on the small of her back, holding her in place. "Can't sit like you're visiting with the Queen. Spread your feet. Center your balance."

She slanted a look at the way he was seated. Inched her boots apart and leaned forward a little. The stool tried rocking for a moment and she muttered something unflattering about the contraption under her breath. But finally, after some shifting and some more heartfelt sighs, she was steady on the small seat.

He took his hand back and fiddled with his reel.

"Hmm. More comfortable than I would have expected."

"Better 'n sitting on the ground," he said.

She was leaning sideways, trying to look at the chair from that angle. "I should have some of these available for guests. They wouldn't take up any significant storage space, and they'd be easy to carry. Even for a child. Nice." Evidently satisfied, she looked at the creek, running about a yard and a half away from their boots. "Now, why is this such a good spot for fishing?"

"Buggers hang out in this narrow neck." Though narrow was a relative term, considering the creek was about thirty feet across at this point. "It's deeper here, but rocky with a lot of plants. Good cover. Plenty of places for them to hide."

"If I relocated the cabins in this area, that would ultimately affect the fishing, wouldn't it?"

"What would you rather do? Give your high-paying guests a spot where they're lucky enough to hook one fish every two months, or chance reducing the fish population? There are still license limits on what can be caught." The irony of his words didn't escape him. She was showing concern over changing the environment and he was advocating the opposite.

"License! I didn't even think about that. I don't have a fishing license and isn't it too late in the year, anyway?"

He smiled slightly, nudging the second rod that lay

on the skiff of snow on the ground between them. "You're not fishing now, are you? Fortunately, this creek is open for fishing year-round. It's not easily navigable by water, and all of your access points are marked No Trespassing, so it's damn near private most of the time." He handed her his rod. "Go ahead. Live dangerously. Hold this."

She made a face, but took the rod from him.

He leaned over and flipped open his tackle box. It was a good thing he could tie a hook blindfolded, given the distraction she presented. In seconds, he'd baited the hook and cast the line for her.

"You make it look easy."

"Doesn't take a master's degree for fishing. Little kids do it. Old people do it. And everyone in between who has the yen. Say the word and I'll show you what to do with one of those worms, there."

She gave a soft laugh. "Nooo, thank you. And I *do* have a master's degree, but I'm still not sure about all this." She pulled the parka zipper halfway down. "You weren't exaggerating when you said it was warm out. I expected it to feel much colder."

"Cloud cover's acting like a blanket." With the toe of his boot, he flipped the lid closed on the tackle box. He'd already shrugged off his coat. It was lying on the ground behind him.

"But you don't think it's going to snow."

"Doesn't smell like it."

She smiled faintly. "Before I came here, I would have dismissed the idea that a person could smell snow before it started falling."

"Give yourself a year or two. You'll be able to sniff

it out on the air, too." If she was still there in a year or two. A month ago, he'd have *wanted* her to be gone. And now? The disturbing thought hung in his head.

He shifted. Moved the tackle box around to prop his boot on it, only to shift again a few minutes later, planting his foot back on the hard ground.

"Ryan could smell snow," he said. And wasn't that a helluva thing that he'd rather think about his son than dwell on whether or not Melanie McFarlane Chilton would be around long enough to cultivate that skill? "Just takes some experience." He jerked out his line long enough to needlessly check the bait and cast it back into the water. "Time was when he loved it out here." Just like Russ had when he'd been a kid.

"But not now?" Her voice was tentative.

His fault. Just like those bruises that had marred her perfect skin were his responsibility.

"He's got a stepfather." As if that explained everything. The years of slowly, unwillingly accepting the fact that Ryan was happier with the man who was there with him every day. Not with the father who'd refused to make his life in the city, the way Nola had wanted. The phone calls he'd made to Ryan. The letters he'd sent that were never answered. The awkward visits he'd made.

He stared at the rippling water. Now all he did was send money. And Nola had wanted him to stop doing even that. They all had Boyd now, after all.

In the middle of summer, the creek was nearly ice-blue in color. Now, it looked nearly black. Greedily swallowing up what light there was, and not giving any of it back out.

"Does he come here to visit you, or do you go there? Or both?"

"Neither. Not anymore." His line suddenly dipped and he rose from the stool, walking down to the water and letting the fish play out for a few minutes before reeling it in. Then he crouched down and caught up the line and the wriggling little trout, and released it again, watching it swim busily deeper until he, too, was swallowed in that dark, winter water.

He returned to the stool, sat down and worked another worm on the hook.

She was watching him and he held up the rod. "You want to try casting this?"

She shook her head. "I'm sorry." She clearly wasn't referring to the fishing pole.

With a flick of his wrist, he sent his line sailing neatly into the deepest portion of the creek. "I'm not going to force my own son to come here and visit me if he doesn't want to come. We fished right here the last time he was here."

"And swam? Where you showed me?"

He exhaled. Nodded, thereby admitting that he hadn't seen his son in three damned years.

Beside him, Melanie shifted slightly. "He's only ten. Maybe those decisions shouldn't be left up to him." She bounced her rod in her hand, making the tip waggle. "I was the GM of McFarlane House Atlanta," she said suddenly. "General manager. I was good at it. Reviews were good. Staff turnover was the lowest it had ever been. Client retention, repeat business, was the highest it had ever been. I'd worked my way up in other locations and when Donovan placed me in Atlanta, I honestly believed that he'd done it because I'd proved myself capable of the position."

He eyed the cheerful little red bobber suspended on her line where it bounced on the surface of the rippling current. "What happened?" He didn't believe for a second that she was incompetent. He'd told her brother that, and he'd surprised himself with the realization that he meant it.

"I found out they were shadowing my managerial decisions." She shifted. Sighed. Set the rod down on the ground beside her chair. "I'd interview a new head for housekeeping. They'd interview the same person right afterward. I'd bring on a new vendor for one thing or another. They'd get hold of the contracts."

"They."

"Donovan. My father. Or Connor. Either one."

"What about your mom? Isn't she involved with the business?"

"She's the CFO. It wasn't as if I were doing anything poorly, either. I wasn't making bad decisions. But they checked up on every single thing I did, anyway. I know it might sound inconsequential to you, but it was…it was—"

"Insulting."

"Yes. I started questioning everything I'd ever thought I was good at." She shook her head. "It was awful."

The bobber on her line dipped for half a second. He looked at her. "You put up with it for two years?"

"I didn't even know about it until last year. I was so confident of myself that it didn't dawn on me to notice the occasional oddity."

"And when you did?"

"I scheduled a meeting with Donovan, of course."

He tried not to snort. This was her father she was talking about, and she had to *schedule* a meeting?

"He didn't even bother trying to deny what they'd been doing. He simply saw nothing wrong with it. As if it were a foregone conclusion that I wasn't capable of making any kind of decisions—minor or major— about the hotel I was running. And then," she pushed to her feet, yanking her coat off all the way and tossing it onto her stool. "*Then,* he had the gall to tell me that I wasn't even guilty of mismanagement. There was nothing *wrong* with anything I'd been doing. He knew it. But did that give him a reason to apologize? To promise to stop?" Her face was indignant as she looked at him. "Of course not! So I turned in my notice. I quit."

"And decided to hightail it to Montana?"

"I'm a McFarlane. I don't hightail it anywhere."

"You're a Chilton now, too, darlin'."

"Not…not *really.*" Her gaze flickered uncertainly before she looked away. "I did a lot of research before I chose Thunder Canyon. Coming here was a very de- liberate act. If I'm going to prove myself, I'm going to do it with the cards stacked in my favor."

So she'd chosen to start up a guest ranch, in an area where she had no friends, no family and no experience.

It still seemed unfathomable to him. But then, the world she'd grown up in was pretty unfathomable.

"Sounds more like you're trying to prove yourself to *you* more than anyone else."

She frowned a little, not answering.

He sighed again. Took a different tack. "Only meetings I ever had with my father were over the dinner table every night."

Her lips curved. She shot him a quick look. "Well. You're the lucky one, then, aren't you?"

He saw the bobber go under and stay in the moment before her unattended rod went skidding off across the wintry grass growing profusely along the edge of the water.

She jumped. "Oh!"

"Well, catch it, Melanie!"

She chased after the rod, barely snagging it by the reel before it went diving straight into the creek. Her boots splashed in the water and she wavered. He lurched forward, too, catching her around the waist before she tumbled forward, right into the water.

She was shaking.

He smoothed his hand down her back, unfortunately conscious of the ridges of her spine and the sweep of her hips in her formfitting blue jeans. "You're all right."

But when she looked over her shoulder at him, it was laughter on her face. Not fear. And she was holding on to the rod with tight hands. "Do I really have a fish?"

Disconcerted, he put his hand over hers on the rod, guiding her fingers to the reel handle. "Reel him in and see."

She turned the reel, retrieving the line, not seeming to care that her expensive leather boots were three inches deep in frigid water or that his hand was still circling her waist, holding her against his body. When he could finally see the fighting trout as she worked it into the shallower water, he reached out and grabbed the line, drawing the fish up and out of the water.

She tossed her head back, her smile wide, her laughter bright. "Isn't he the most beautiful thing?"

And everything inside Russ seemed to stop in its tracks. He looked at her. The expensive redhead with East in her voice, looking more alive and vibrant than he'd ever seen her. All because of a thirteen-inch rainbow trout.

"You want to keep him?" What he wanted to do was keep her.

And that was as unlikely as wishing things were different with Ryan.

She shook her head. "Lord, no. He's not going to be hurt, is he?"

Russ shook his head and lowered the fish into the water where he worked the hook free, his fingers almost immediately numb from the cold. In seconds the fish disappeared.

He straightened. Wiped his hands down his jeans and took a long step back up onto dry land.

Her eyes were still sparkling. "You didn't tell me it was like this."

"Like what?" His voice was gruff, but she didn't seem to notice.

"Perfect." She lifted her hands to her sides. "Absolutely, wonderfully perfect."

And laughing, she carried the rod back to the tripod stool, tossed aside her coat, and sat back down. When she reached for the container of worms and gave him an expectant solve-this-for-me look, he knew he was a goner.

Hook. Line. Sinker.

Chapter Fourteen

Melanie knew the afternoon was passing, though she couldn't have told it by the cast of the sun, which was well hidden behind the veil of clouds.

She couldn't recall feeling more contented in her life and knew that it wasn't just the stream, or the fishing tackle, or the lone trout that she'd hooked.

It was the company.

Russ didn't return to the subject of Ryan, and she didn't push. They'd already told one another more than she would ever have expected, particularly considering the distance that had been between them the past few days.

So they sat there, side by side.

When he showed her how to cast, she moved down the shoreline a little ways from him and practiced. And finally, she managed not to have the line plopping almost directly in front of her feet, but could send it sailing in a beautiful arc right into the middle of the stream.

"You'd be good at fly-fishing," he told her.

She didn't want to examine the pleasure that swept through her too closely because she doubted that it had all that much to do with the notion of fly-fishing— oddly and unexpectedly appealing as that was—but had far more to do with the man making the comment.

"Nobody back in Philadelphia will believe it when I tell them." She drew in the line and prepared to cast it out again. There was no hook. No bait. Just a weird, rubbery weight that he'd tied to the end of her line for practicing.

"Need a photograph to show them. Could have shot one of you if you had your cell phone around. Seems like they all have cameras on them these days."

"I gave up my cell phone months ago." The line zipped out with a satisfying whiz, seemed to hover in the air for a moment, then dropped neatly into the current. "I'll bet this is even better when it's really warm outside."

"Why didn't you say so before?"

She didn't pretend to misunderstand. "It's just a cell phone. Not very important. Nobody calls me, anyway, and if they do, they can reach me on the landline at the house."

"I thought I was the only one who didn't bother with cell phones."

She smiled faintly. "Now you know you're not. See how much we have in common?" she added dryly.

"What about your friends?"

"I had business associates. Not friends." A drop of water hit her nose, and she jerked, startled, thinking that it was creek water somehow splashing up on her. But when it was followed by another drop, smacking her cheek, she looked up. "I think—" she caught a raindrop on her eyelid "—it's raining."

"You're a smart woman. Can't you come up with a better excuse to get out of putting real bait on that line?"

"I'm not making any excuses about that," she assured. This fishing thing was the most fun she'd had in ages, but she wasn't foolish enough to think worms were the only kind of bait that a person could use. "I'll shovel all the horse manure you want, I'll pick crud out of horseshoes, I'll even clean toilets. But I am not sticking my fingers in that cup of oozing worms." She dashed her hand across her cheek. "And it most certainly *is* raining."

He glanced up, finally, and squinted into the thick, gray sky just as it seemed to pull the plug and let loose a deluge. "Oh, damn." He jumped up, knocking over his tripod seat, and jogged toward her, grabbing her arm, even as she was already turning and making her own dash for the shelter of his old orange truck.

The water came down in heavy sheets, turning the thin layer of snow underneath their feet to slippery mush.

Melanie thought, too late, of their coats, still lying by the abandoned stools and fishing tackle, but then they'd made it to the truck parked at the top of the creek bank and Russ's wet hand slid over hers as they simultaneously reached for the door handle.

He pulled open the door, virtually lifting her onto the seat, and shoved himself in right after her.

He dragged the door closed and shook his head like a wet dog.

Even more water flew over her, and she laughed. "Stop!"

His teeth flashed wickedly. But he stopped. "Are you okay?"

She slicked her hands through her bedraggled hair, pushing it back from her face. "It's just rain. I'm not likely to melt."

"Might freeze," he murmured. He reached past her and turned the key in the ignition, started up the truck and directed the heater vents toward her.

It was true. She'd been comfortably cool without her coat while she'd been laboring with the fishing pole. But now, she was simply shivering.

And the vents weren't warming up anywhere near quickly enough. She rubbed her hands together in front of one of the vents and looked out at their useless coats. "I'm thinking that forgetting the coats probably wasn't the smartest move we've ever made."

"Probably not." He flicked a few buttons on his thick, flannel shirt and pulled it over his head, handing it to her. "Put that on."

She gulped a little at the sight of the snug cotton undershirt he'd revealed, but nevertheless pulled the shirt over her own head. It was only slightly damp around the shoulders, and it smelled wonderfully of him. She barely managed to keep herself from burying her nose in the voluminous folds. "Thank you."

He pulled her close to him, rubbing his hands bracingly up and down her back, warming her through the layers. "It'll warm up in a sec."

Every nerve inside her felt poised for danger, yet she ignored all the warning signs. Her hands went from clutching the collar of his shirt together at her throat to the solid heat of his chest. "I'm sorry."

"For what?"

"The rain."

He pulled his head back, peering at her suspiciously though there was a faint smile playing around his lips. "Why? What'd you do? A rain dance?"

"Hardly. But we were out here because of me."

"It's just a little rain." His voice dropped. "Didn't have to hold a gun to my head to get me out here, Melanie. If anything, I remember pulling you out the door."

She swallowed. He so rarely called her by her name.

He let out a low laugh that sounded pained. "I'm having enough trouble keeping my mind away from where it shouldn't be without you looking at me like that again."

She realized she was staring at his lips and hurriedly looked away. "Like what?"

He wrapped his hand around her face and nudged her chin upward. "Like this—" he slowly dragged his thumb over her lower lip "—is what you want."

Her heart lurched, crowding up into her throat.

It *was* what she wanted.

But every time she tried to tell him that, he backed away. Called a halt. No matter what he said, what reasons he gave, she just ended up feeling foolish.

And if there was one thing Melanie hated, it was feeling as if she didn't know what she was doing, with everyone in sight witnessing it. With *him* witnessing it.

"Russ—" Her lips brushed against his thumb as she murmured his name.

His other hand, still on her back, slowed its comforting, bracing strokes. And it felt as if she could feel every centimeter of each finger, splayed, hot, through her sweater, through her spine, through her flesh, into her bloodstream that seemed to rush through her, hotter, pooling yet again in the very center of her.

Thunder rumbled around them and the rain sounded loud as it pounded on the roof of the truck, streaming down the windows, blurring the view of the land. The meandering creek.

His eyes seemed to darken by degrees. "Here we are again."

She moistened her lips. "I don't mind." The admission was little more than a whisper, but he still managed to hear it, despite the vibrating, pounding rain around them.

Pounding that was echoed by the blood pulsing inside her veins.

"That's the problem, darlin'. Just tell me you don't want this and it'll be okay." He reached for the handle. "I'll grab the gear and I'll drive you back."

"Wait." A shudder worked through her, and he had to feel it, pressed together the way they were. She'd been telling herself that she didn't want this—with anyone—for so long she'd thought it was ingrained in her. "I…can't."

His hand rested on the door latch. His jaw canted, slightly off-center, the edge of his teeth meeting for a moment. "Can't?"

"Can't tell you that," she whispered.

The breath he drew in filled his chest, pressing it even more firmly against her curves. "I didn't get you out here for this."

"I know." She shivered again. When had her hands worked themselves around his waist? "You wanted me to understand a little more about *your* Thunder Canyon." It wasn't just about fishing. It went much deeper."

She understood that.

His gaze was on her mouth. "Yeah."

She touched the tip of her tongue to her upper lip but the moisture just as quickly evaporated by the heat blazing in his eyes. "I'm glad," she whispered. "That you showed me. That. Out there." Not entirely certain where her nerve came from, she covered his hand on the door latch and drew it away. Held it to her breast, over her racing heart. "Show me more. Right here."

His fingers flexed beneath her hand. Grazed her breasts. Made her mind spiral and spin.

"You're probably used to five-hundred-dollar sheets and expensive champagne."

Not in the way he thought. "Does it matter?"

"We'll go back to the house," he murmured.

"No." She was afraid if they did, he'd change his mind. Or she'd change hers.

That common sense would prevail over at least one of them, and she didn't think she could bear it to get this close to him again and not get as close as two people could get. "I don't want to wait. I just want—"

He covered her mouth, swallowing the *you* that was little more than a moan.

And just that easily, it wasn't the wet cold that had her shivering. It was the heat of him that made her tremble, that made her sigh and feel flushed in a way that she'd never before felt.

With the water pouring around them, he slowly drew his shirt back off her head and dropped it on the dashboard. When his fingers went to her hair, sliding it once more away from her face, she closed her eyes, pressing her forehead for a breathless moment against his palm that had impossible tears pricking dangerously behind her eyes.

But then he moved again and pushed his hands beneath the hem of her sweater, pulling it off. The feel of his hands against her bare skin made her haul in a shaking breath, particularly when he lay his palm over her ribs covering the worst of her bruises.

"Does it still hurt?" His voice was low. Hushed.

She shook her head. "N-not much." What hurt was the pulsing, yawning emptiness inside her. The distance, even just the few inches, that separated them. The slow, deliberate glide of his thumb against the thin pink fabric of her bra, circling above, below, around the tight crest that begged for contact.

He shifted on the seat, cursing under his breath at the confining space. "I'm telling you, sweetheart, there's more space just five miles away—"

She reached between her breasts and flipped open the small clasp holding the bra cups together. They sprang apart, still partly caught around her flesh.

"—from here," he finished, suddenly sounding a little strangled as he touched one of the cups. Just a bare graze, and it slid aside farther, revealing one tight, rosy nipple. His eyes seemed to pinpoint a little.

She took that as a good sign and wriggled her shoulders until the narrow pink straps slid down her upper **arms and caught there. By some small miracle she** managed to toe off her boots, and she turned toward him, slipping one leg over his thighs until she sat in his lap, facing him.

He closed his eyes for a moment, but his hands slid down her hips, fingers kneading into her flesh, causing all manner of clanging inside her nerves.

Then he pulled her up onto her knees and lowered his head until he could press his mouth against the vividly shaded yellow and green still coloring her rib cage.

She gasped and twined her arms around his shoulders. His neck. Ran her fingers through the thick, damp strands of his hair as his mouth slowly, interminably slowly, worked its way upward until he touched his tongue against one hard, peaked nipple.

She bit back a whimper, but couldn't contain another when he covered her other breast in his hand, raking his calloused palm against that equally needy point.

And then his mouth was leaving her nipple, wet and tingling as he dragged his lips up the valley between her breasts. Stopped to torment the pulse beating at the base of her throat, and finally—oh, God, finally he found her mouth once again.

He dragged her bra straps off her arms and tossed the thing aside. Their fingers were suddenly bumping between them as she dragged at his T-shirt and he pulled at the button on her waistband. He finally laughed, short, deep, and not really amused, and ripped his T-shirt over his head himself. "Unfasten your jeans."

Quaking inside, she fumbled with the button. The zipper. And evidently she wasn't quick enough to suit him, because he finally took over the job himself and worked them down over her hips as far as they could go. "Finish," he bade tersely.

But there wasn't demand in his expression. Only the same kind of driving desperation that was fueling her own motions.

So she pushed awkwardly up onto her knees, bumped her head against the roof of the cab and worked off one leg. Then the other. And then she was just hovering over him wearing nothing at all but the panties that matched her pink bra.

"For three weeks now," he slid a finger over her hip where the narrow strap connected the minuscule triangles of fabric together, "I've been living with the memory of you that morning. When we left Grant's resort. When I knew you weren't wearing anything at all beneath that soft red dress."

His finger slid beneath the strap, and she lost the ability to breathe, before he slid his finger slowly back out again.

"I might as well have been a thirteen-year-old kid for the way that tormented me," he admitted.

Another rushing, heated wave coursed through her. "Russ—"

He exhaled, long and hard. Yet the way he turned his hand, brushed his knuckles along the elastic edge of her panties across her abdomen, was nothing but gentle.

Her abdomen jerked when he reached the front and grazed his fingertips against the fabric. Against *her.*

When he turned his hand again and pressed his palm there, her head fell forward, finding his shoulder.

And when that palm slid between her thighs, seared

through the thin veil of silk to the center of her that wept just for him, it was the hard smooth flesh of his broad shoulder that stifled the cry that rose in her.

He made a low sound and caught her behind her back, holding her steady even as that delving, tormenting palm stroked and cajoled and all too quickly sent her nerves screaming through the roof as she convulsed endlessly against him.

"That's what I've dreamed about," he murmured when she finally collapsed against him. "You. Coming apart in my hands."

She couldn't have formed a coherent word to save her soul.

Her heart was still thudding. The rain was still pounding.

And she was still wanting.

She worked her shaking hands between them and tugged at the belt buckle that was digging into her belly.

He drew in a hissing breath and his hands fell away from her.

She ought to have been cold given the hazy realization that the engine wasn't running anymore. He must have turned it off at some point, but the windows were fogged with warmth.

She sat back a few inches on his legs and, tucking the tip of her tongue between her teeth, set to work on his belt in earnest. The metal buckle jingled when she finally slid the ends free. And then hesitancy hit her, faced with the very strained fly of his jeans.

Flushing, procrastinating slightly, she turned herself around until she could lean over his legs and reach his boots, which came off much less easily than hers had.

And when she heard his strangled chuckle, she looked over her shoulder at him. "What?"

He just shook his head, looking pained. "Honey, you have no idea." He rubbed his hands down her bare bottom and set her off his lap, finally managing to shove off the boots himself. Angling his long, wide body back against the door, he yanked his fly apart, the buttons seeming to pop as they escaped their confines.

And then his golden-brown eyes pinned her in place. "Well?"

She swallowed. Looked at him, but didn't look at him, because if she did he'd surely realize that there were better women than she at this whole thing. She put her trembling hands on the lower portion of his jeans where she could get a good purchase, and pulled as he lifted his hips.

And suddenly, the jeans and his plain navy boxers beneath came free of his hips and she fell back, knocking her elbow against the steering wheel. The very sight of him made her breathless.

The corner of his lip lifted lazily, wickedly, sending a clenching jolt right down to her soul. "*Next* time, it'll be in a bed. A big—" he tugged the clothing out of her nonresistant fingers and tossed them onto the floor with the rest of their clothing "—wide—" he closed his hands around her upper arms and urged her toward him "—bed." His mouth found hers once again as he leaned back against the door, pulling her nearly prone over him.

Barely able to contemplate the "next time" when she wasn't sure her senses could survive this time, she moaned, and somehow he was there, right there, nudging against her, begging entry. And she knew that she should tell him—tell him that she was probably no good at this, that she didn't know enough—but the words just wouldn't come, wouldn't break free. Couldn't break free because there was no room with the gasping cry that welled inside her throat as he closed his hands over her thighs, pulling them alongside his. Then her body didn't care about her lack of experience. Her ignorance. It simply took over, arching against him, taking him deep inside.

She gave a sharp cry and stiffened for only a moment, rapidly accustoming to the unfamiliar invasion, particularly with the way his hands swept over her, pulling her tighter to him.

"You've gotta be kidding me," he growled.

And she realized with a suddenly cold pang that his hands weren't urging her onward.

They were like iron, holding her still.

She blinked against the fog of need clouding her brain.

"You're a *virgin?*" His voice rose, incredulously.

She felt the flush rise through her, an entirely strange sensation completely at odds with the heat still streaking through her from the still very noticeable union between them. She tilted her chin a little. "Not anymore." The muscles deep inside her flexed spasmodically.

His teeth bared. "Stop that."

"If I could, I would," she whispered, helplessly in the grip of that pulsing, aching need for him.

A low, long rumble of thunder rolled over them, deep and sonorous.

And then he swore, bowing against her even as he seemed to try to hold her away.

But there was no distance anymore between them. And instead of pushing her away, his hands were closing around her, lifting her, pulling her, urging her. Deeper, faster, a headlong rush into fathoms of absolutely perfect ecstasy that had him groaning her name, again and again, in the moments before her senses exploded yet again.

And after, the only thing she was aware of was the way he dragged his flannel shirt over her back. Of his arms that surrounded her, holding her close against him as their hearts slowed and exhausted, of spent tears sliding silently down her cheek, disappearing into the swirl of dark hair on his chest where her head was cradled.

Chapter Fifteen

The rain was still pouring down around their truck when Russ finally pulled on his jeans and T-shirt. He didn't dare watch Melanie too closely as she fumbled her way into her own clothing, or he'd be dragging her back down on the seat and having his way with her all over again.

Hardly the behavior a virgin was used to.

He pinched the bridge of his nose for a long minute, trying to get rid of the pain pulsing there.

A virgin.

How the hell had *that* happened? Or more to the specific point, how the hell had that *not* happened?

"You're thirty years old." The words came out of him.

She paused in the act of reaching for her panties where they were caught over the edge of the brake pedal and gave him a look like a startled doe. Then she blinked and snatched up the scrap of pink silk. "So?" Her voice was defensive.

The pain in his head throbbed a little harder, vying for supremacy over the pain that throbbed inside him considerably farther south. "So…why me? Why now?"

She lifted her shoulder. "Why not?" She was probably trying for flippancy, but she failed miserably. "You *are* my husband." Not looking at him, she hurriedly slipped the panties up her legs, managing to look elegant despite their ridiculously cramped quarters. She'd pushed her arms through the sleeves of his flannel shirt, and the shirt tails hung well down her thighs and with one of those quick motions that only women seemed able to master, pulled up her drawers without managing to reveal an extra inch of skin.

He shoved his fingers through his hair, annoyed with proof of what a dog he was when he recognized his disappointment. As if he really *were* a thirteen-year-old kid, thwarted from seeing a little more length of taut, creamy female thigh.

"Don't worry," she said, and her voice was as chilled as the air slowly creeping around the edges of the doors. "Nothing's changed. You'll still get your half of the Hopping H as agreed."

"What? I don't get another percentage for services rendered?"

She shot him a pained look. "Must you be vile?"

Evidently, he must. He leaned over and yanked on his boots, thwacking his forehead on the dashboard in the process. "God*dammit.*"

She jumped.

And he wanted to swear a lot more loudly and a whole lot worse. He jammed his bootlaces into the top of the boots, not bothering to tie them, and sat up. "Scoot over me."

She looked warily at him.

"Unless *you* want to drive back to the H," he added pointedly, since she was sitting behind the wheel.

Her answer was clear in the way she gingerly crawled over his thighs, keeping contact to a bare minimum as if she might contract cooties if she got to close. He considered telling her that as far as that went, she'd been exposed about as thoroughly as a woman could be exposed.

Which just had another thought shooting through him, leaving cold panic in its wake. "We didn't use anything."

She was now working her sweater on, and still doing it beneath cover of his flannel shirt. Quite an interesting feat, actually. "What?" Her voice was muffled.

He let out an impatient breath. "Protection."

Her head popped back up through the open neck of his shirt. With just a few brushes of her fingers, her silky hair slid back into its well-cut lines.

She didn't look as if she'd taken a rain-soaked roll around the confines of a truck cab at all.

Except for the color riding high in her cheeks, she didn't look much different than she had before they'd set out earlier that day. Only she *was* different now, thanks to his monumental lack of self-control.

"Protection," he repeated brusquely.

Her eyes widened as if such a thought had never occurred to her. "Oh."

He wrapped his hands around the steering wheel. It was safer than her tempting body and marginally wiser than his own neck. "For two seemingly intelligent adults, we've managed to really muck it up."

"I'm not going to get pregnant," she assured swiftly.

He just eyed her. "It only takes once, sweetheart."

Her expression flickered with realization. "I suppose you know that from experience?"

"Pretty much." Nola had stopped taking her birth control pills right after their wedding night. Of course, he hadn't known that then. He'd learned that after the fact, when she announced she was pregnant just a few short months later. And then used the pregnancy as a reason why they should move back to the bosom of her family. In Boston. From then on, it had been a never-ending war to change him into the kind of man she really wanted.

"Your son was a mistake?"

"Ryan was unexpected," he corrected evenly. "Never a mistake."

"Then why don't you still try to see him?"

"Just because we've slept together doesn't mean I want to hear your opinion on matters that don't concern you."

She reared back as if he'd slapped her.

And damned if he felt as if he might as well have. But she'd delivered her own wallop to him already, in the form of her virginity.

He cranked the engine over and was glad when it chugged back to life. He flipped on the heater and reached for the door. "Wait here." He shut the door on the where-would-I-go? look that she gave him and jogged, slipping and sliding, down the increasingly slick bank to retrieve their sopping coats and the tackle. He grabbed it all up in one load, then hauled his freezing ass back up the hill where he dumped everything in the truck bed.

He was soaked when he got behind the wheel again. Soaked and cold down to the bone.

Finally cold enough not to be afraid that one touch from her would have him jumping her bones all over again.

A virgin.

The words rolled around inside his head as he turned the truck in a wide circle and hit the gas, taking the most direct path back to the Hopping H, rather than reversing the route he'd used to get there.

It was a helluva lot more bumpy.

But it was a helluva lot shorter.

Within ten minutes or so, the outbuildings were in sight. And then the big, comfortable-looking house.

He pulled up in the rear. "Get inside. Take a warm bath or something. You don't want to catch a cold."

She huffed. "You're the one sitting there in a puddle of icy water. Not me." But she pushed open the truck door and, ducking her head against the elements, hurried up the back steps, disappearing inside.

Russ grimaced. Shut off the engine without realizing he intended to, and followed her into the house. She must have already gone upstairs, because there was no sight of her in the big, gleaming kitchen. She wasn't sitting at her improvised desk, and the great room was empty.

He headed up the stairs, not caring a hell of a lot that he was trailing water with every step. He stomped down the hall, ignored the partially opened door to her bedroom and continued on to his where he stripped out of his wet clothes and left them in a heap on the braided area rug. The sight of the neat stack of towels on his dresser was a welcome surprise and he grabbed one off the top, hitching it around his hips before stomping back down the hall to the bathroom.

She was in there, standing in front of the sink, her shoulders slumped.

He stopped short.

Her gaze lifted to his in the mirror and he knew he was the one responsible for the wariness he saw there. "You can use the bath connected to your room now," she reminded.

He gripped the rich, chocolate-brown towel at his waist. So much for the aftereffects of a winter rainstorm.

If she hadn't been a virgin, he would have dropped the towel right then and there and convinced her that being lovers wouldn't put a bad twist on their unlikely marriage.

But she *had* been.

She hadn't told him. And he was plenty pissed about that particular fact.

He was also scared witless because knowing that he'd been her first…her only…mattered more than he wanted to acknowledge.

The whole thing was ridiculous. They were told old for this kind of foolishness. Too cynical. Too…everything.

"Would you mind not staring at me?" she asked stiffly.

He turned on his heel and headed back to his bedroom where he shut the door with more force than was necessary.

He went into the adjoining bathroom, seeing for the first time the work that had been completed in the past few days. Expensive-looking natural stone tiles. Gleaming steel and polished, ebony wood.

All very nice and he couldn't care less as he reached around the glass block wall that took the place of a shower door or curtain and turned on the water.

Cold.

When he was relatively certain that he was on the verge of frostbite, he let the water warm just enough so he didn't feel as if he had ice crystals forming on his skin, and stepped back out of the shower. He pulled on dry clothes, then snatched up his wet shirt and jeans and flipped them over the top of the glass block, and left the bathroom.

Only to turn back a moment later. He grabbed his jeans, fished in the back pocket and pulled out the folded prenuptial napkin. Even it was damp. He carefully opened the fold, revealing their scrawled signatures, and left it on the dresser to dry.

This time, when he went downstairs through the great room, Melanie was at her desk. Listening to phone messages and making notes on her pad.

She didn't give him so much as a glance.

And he felt even *more* annoyed, which he knew wasn't really the mark of a grown man. He went into the kitchen and pushed some buttons on the fancy coffee-maker she'd gotten but never used for herself and threw together a thick ham sandwich that he wolfed down with a scalding coffee chaser as if he hadn't eaten in days.

When he passed by her again, she was still buried in

her notepads, the telephone tucked between her shoulder and her ear. "I'll be sure to remind him, Steph. Thanks." She dropped the phone in its cradle. "That was Stephanie," she stated the obvious when he stopped in the middle of the room.

"And? I've already picked up the danged suit she wants me to wear. What else is she worrying about now?"

Melanie's gaze was cool. As standoffish as it had been the very first time he'd come face-to-face with her all those months ago. "She said to remind you about the Cowboy Christmas Ball on Saturday."

He'd forgotten all about it. Every year whoever was around from the old crowd headed out for the big do that was held in the old Town Hall downtown. There was no way his friends wouldn't be expecting to see him there this year, with his new bride on his arm. "I suppose we should show our faces there." His jaw ached. "For appearances and all."

Her lips firmed. "Of course. Is it black-tie?"

He snorted. "Not in this lifetime, princess. This is Thunder Canyon, remember? Not one of your swanky celebrity-attended McFarlane events."

"Then what is the expected dress?"

He propped his hands on the desk and leaned over her. "Consider it research. You can learn something from the event about what people *really* want for entertainment around this place versus fancy equipment like that—" he waved his hand in the direction of the media room "—and fancy parties like you are used to."

She made a face at him. *"Attire?"*

He let out a harsh breath. "String ties for the guys,

if any tie at all. And purdy little dresses for the fillies. Wear jeans. Wear a skirt. Wear whatever the hell you want as long as you've got cowboy boots on your feet."

She absorbed that, looking a little discomfited by the idea.

"You *do* have boots by now, don't you?"

"Yes. I bought a pair months ago."

For all he knew, they'd be turquoise leather and rhinestone-studded. "Good. Food starts around seven. Drinking and everything else at seven-oh-five. Think you can manage to be ready on time this time?"

"I can if you can." She looked down at her notepad, seeming to dismiss him.

He straightened. "I'll be at the J for the next few days."

"Indeed." She flipped a few pages and made more notes. "What else is new? I do expect you to hold to your end of our agreement, you know. It's like you pointed out already. Just because we've slept together doesn't mean that anything else has changed. You have your business. I have mine."

"And only the twain of the Hopping H shall have us meet."

"Isn't that the way you prefer it? As long as you stick to your end, I'll stick to mine."

He glared at the top of her head. Her red head. "Be careful when you go out," he answered instead. "The rain'll have melted the snow and when it all freezes back up again, there's gonna be ice everywhere."

"Fine." Her voice was blithe.

"Fine," he returned, and headed out the front door, grabbing his spare oilskin duster off the peg as he went. Oh, yeah. He really hated the word *fine*.

Because there was nothing fine about anything. Nothing at all.

The moment the front door thudded shut after Russ, Melanie tossed down her pen and lowered her head to her trembling hands.

Why on earth had she ever let herself believe that becoming intimate with Russ would work on any level?

He obviously regretted it.

Just as her worst fears had warned her. There was a reason why she'd avoided personal relationships all of these years, and now she had the evidence to back it all up.

When it came to such matters, she was a miserable failure.

She groaned, trying to block out the too vivid, too recent memory of the way she'd wantonly thrown herself at Russ, and nearly jumped out of her skin when the phone jangled noisily beside her. She scrubbed her hands down her scorching cheeks, then picked it up. "Melanie McFarlane."

"Hello, Miss McFarlane. This is Jane from Connor McFarlane's office."

As if she wouldn't know her own brother's secretary? "How can I help you, Jane?"

"I'm just calling with your travel arrangements," Jane said, ever bright, and reeled off the flight information.

"No return flight?"

"Oh. No, ma'am. Connor said it was one-way."

Of course he had. "Thank you, Jane."

"Have a safe trip home," the other woman finished, before disconnecting.

"*This* is home," Melanie said to the dial tone as she hung up her end and eyed the flight and time that she'd written down. Departing Sunday. The day before Christmas, and the day following the Cowboy Christmas Ball.

She sighed again and shoved aside the notepad.

It teetered, then fell off the edge of the desk, and she just let it lie there. Uncaring.

All around her, the house was still and silent. No sounds of the rain penetrating the sturdy walls of this place, though she could see through the windows lining the front of the great room that it was still falling. Steadily.

Ordinarily, when the loneliness of the house started to get to her, she was able to envision the place filled with the lively noise of happy guests. Of children scrabbling across the wood floor, of adults talking, glasses clinking.

It was all like music to her.

Only now, the music was silent.

And it was all her fault for trying to reach out for more than she already had.

She was a McFarlane.

And McFarlanes were never any good with the people they loved.

The realization that she placed Russ within that particular group wasn't so much a lightning bolt as a pit of quicksand into which she'd long ago sunk.

She wasn't even sure when.

She just knew that she had.

She was in love with her husband. In love with Russ Chilton, and *that* was why she'd taken that monumental leap of making love with him.

It wasn't a lifetime of unexpressed, bottled sexual energy.

It was *him*. The one man who, in just the few short weeks of their convenient marriage, had made her start to believe in herself again. Who'd started to convince her that she wasn't weak. Or incompetent. Or foolish.

Only now, he was virtually running for the hills, all because she'd mistakenly let herself believe that maybe, just maybe, he'd wanted her as desperately as she wanted him.

Well, if he had, the moment had clearly passed, thanks to the reality of making love with her.

She would have been better off sticking to mucking out stalls and trying to decipher the old ranch records than trying to seduce her husband into losing his head— if not his heart—just as thoroughly as she already had.

Much better off.

She dragged herself up the stairs, wincing slightly at the pull of muscles that were never before used. She went into the bathroom and ran the warm bath Russ had recommended.

But when she climbed out of the swirling, bubbling water a long while later, her eyes aching from the weak tears she'd finally let fall amid the rushing noise of the jetted water, and dried herself off, she pulled the soft, navy flannel shirt of his right back over her head.

And then, despite the cloudy daylight that was still clinging to the horizon, she climbed into her sleigh bed and pulled the covers over her head.

Maybe it was childish.

But the aching inside her heart didn't feel childish at all.

It just felt wounded. And empty.

Chapter Sixteen

Melanie had been in the Town Hall located in the older section of Thunder Canyon a few times since she'd moved to Montana, each time to attend a town meeting where, more often than not, she'd witnessed Russ stating his case against one thing or another, be it zoning or curfews.

But now the big building with the awning stretching all the way across its Western-style front looked much more festive than it had for any of the town meetings.

Tiny white lights were strung all around the awning and enormous boughs of balsam, festooned with red berries and ribbons, hung from the wooden railing that bordered the neatly swept wooden walkway. And as Melanie and Russ approached the hall from across the town square, where they'd finally found an available parking space, she could hear the music coming out of the building whenever someone pulled open the front door, going in or out.

"That doesn't sound like Christmas music to me," she murmured to Russ, who was striding along so fast she practically had to skip to keep up with him. And skipping in her thoroughly unfamiliar cowboy boots was probably not the best of ideas, given the slick condition of the ground beneath them and the light smattering of snowflakes falling on top of it.

He'd been right about the rain and the resulting ice once the temperature dropped again. Which it had done just the previous day, plunging lower than she'd ever experienced. And then, that afternoon, gentle snow flurries had begun.

Now, the ice seemed everywhere. She'd slid and fallen too many times to count at the Hopping H while she'd gone about taking care of the chores she *could* handle.

"It's a waltz," he told her, grabbing her elbow through her fur coat and helping her across the people-congested street in front of the hall. "Presumably you know how to do that."

She pulled her elbow out of his grasp the moment she was certain nobody could see. "Do *you?*"

"Don't sound so shocked." He pulled open the door and waited for her to go inside. "There was a time my mother tried to teach me some couth. We do that even here in Thunder Canyon."

She stopped in her tracks, disregarding the flow of people around them. "If you're going to toss around insults all evening, I'd just as soon go back home."

Since the day they'd gone fishing—she refused to think about the far more momentous happenings of that particular day—their only conversations had been about ranch matters. Put in an order for wire fencing. Get the vet out to check the pregnant mares. Reschedule delivery of a load of hay.

Because of her foolishness, they'd managed to take a giant step backward in dealing with one another. It was as tense as it had been upon their first meeting, when he'd made no bones about his disapproval of her presence in Thunder Canyon.

Only now it was worse, because in the beginning she'd naively believed that he hadn't really meant that personally. How could he have, when they didn't even know one another?

Now, they knew one another, in the truest sense of that word. And he very clearly meant things. Personally.

"I've never insinuated that people here lacked class." She kept her voice low. For his ears only. "You're the one who seems to have a bug in his bonnet about it."

"Hey there, Russ." A slender, hazel-eyed blonde hailed him. She hardly looked dressed for a Christmas ball in her heavy brown trousers and slick, weatherproof coat. "I hear congratulations are in order."

Russ's smile was tight. "Faith Stevenson," he introduced. "She runs the search and rescue team here. Faith, this is my…wife. Melanie."

Search and rescue. Melanie realized that probably explained the woman's attire. She was on duty. "It's a pleasure to meet you, Faith." She extended her hand to the other woman. This was Erik Stevenson's stepmother. The one with whom Russ had gone to school.

Faith returned her handshake, her eyes sparkling. Everything about her seemed golden, from the top of her long, gleaming blond hair to her smoothly tanned face. "I didn't think I'd see the day when Russ here would settle down again. I hope you'll be very happy together." Her lips tilted mischievously. "He's a good guy, despite rumors to the contrary."

"Nice," Russ muttered. "Where's Cam?"

"He's supposed to be around here somewhere." Faith waived her hand. "Chasing down Erik, undoubtedly." She looked at Melanie. "Cam is my husband," she elaborated. "Our son, Erik, has an amazing ability to find mischief where there ordinarily should be none. He tends to keep us on our toes." She pulled an official-looking radio off her heavy-duty belt when it crackled. "I'm just off duty," she told them. "That fortunately ended well. But I've still got to go make my report. Hopefully I'll catch up with you all later." She looked at Melanie again. "Good luck with the Hopping H. I think having a guest ranch around here is a fabulous idea." Smiling brightly, she squeezed Russ's arm and slipped through a group of people just coming in through the doorway.

"Did you date her?"

"What?" Russ looked at her as if she'd lost her mind, and she wished she could retract the embarrassing question. "No, I did not *date* her." He grabbed her coat and left it, along with his, at the old-fashioned coat check, then took her arm and ushered her through the teeming lobby, through another door and into a high, wide room was filled to the rafters with the sounds and scents of Christmas. "I told you about Erik. He's the one who found the gold nugget that set this town on its ear again with an infernal gold rush. He fell into an abandoned mine. Faith was the one to find him. Pull him out."

Feeling chastised, Melanie adjusted the pink silk scarf draped around the waist of her long black broomstick skirt. "She sounds remarkable."

"She is." His voice was short.

And Melanie was thoroughly *un*remarkable. "How old is Erik?"

"Nine." His gaze grew shuttered, and she knew he wasn't thinking of Erik Stevenson but of his own son. And there, surrounded by all of the Christmas frippery and the raised voices of people hailing one another, it struck her as unrelentingly sad that Russ wasn't having to chase after his own adventuresome boy.

"Why don't you call Ryan?" The impetuous question burst out of her, just proving that whatever self-control she might have once possessed was thoroughly absent without leave. "Just talk to him. It's so obvious that you want to."

His heavy brows pulled together in annoyance. "Melanie—"

"I'm just asking! Suggesting!"

His hand tightened around the long sleeve of her snug black knit top as he pretty much pushed her through the tightly arranged tables that filled the perimeter of the room, stopping first at the outlandishly generous buffet tables where he filled her plate to overflowing. "There's Grant and Steph," he pointed out. "Looks like there are a few seats left at their table. Try and pretend you're crazy in love with me, if you wouldn't mind? I'd just as soon we not be a downer on everyone else's holiday."

She swallowed. *Try?*

"Got a few spare seats?" he asked Grant when they reached the table.

"Saving 'em for you," Grant assured. His gaze seemed disturbingly perceptive as he took in the two of them. "Everyone else is already here. Wasn't sure you guys were going to make it." He rose and pulled out the spare chair for Melanie as if he suspected that Russ wasn't going to do the honors.

Melanie sent him a small smile and set her full plate on the table as she sat down in the cool metal folding chair. There was obviously no set dinner hour, because the others had plates in front of them, as well, all in various stages of their meal. Across from them, Mia Cates was deep in conversation with Lizbeth Stanton and Allaire Traub, the fragile-looking blonde whose photograph had been in the paper recently when she'd married D.J. Traub, her one-time brother-in-law and the owner of a successful barbecue restaurant chain. They barely broke conversation long enough to send distracted greetings to Melanie and Russ before ducking their heads together once more.

Her fingers toyed with her plastic fork, but she knew she would be hard-pressed to actually eat anything.

She was simply too tense.

Russ, on the other hand, had immediately tucked into a fried chicken leg as he struck up conversation with Dax Traub on the other side of him.

Melanie looked over at Steph, who was sitting on the other side of Grant. "How are the wedding plans?" Steph looked pretty as a picture with her hair tied back with a red ribbon that matched her red Western-cut blouse.

"Everything's right on track," she told her, leaning across Grant slightly to be heard above the band that was now cranking out a raucous version of "Jingle Bells." "Grant's mother, Helen, and his sister, Elise, will be in from Billings tomorrow morning, and they'll help finish up the last few tasks." She smiled. "I don't know what we were thinking, planning the wedding for Christmas Day!"

Grant slid his arm over her shoulder. "We were thinking it was the best present either one of us could ever have."

Melanie had to look away from the way Steph's gaze melted. Only she encountered Russ's gaze on *her* face when she did so.

His expression grim, he shoved back from the chair that he'd barely sat in at all, and her stomach dropped to her toes. Did he want to leave when they'd just arrived?

But he merely wiped his hands with the napkin that he dropped on top of the table and stuck out his hand to her expectantly. "Let's dance."

Then her stomach lurched around with an entirely different kind of panic. Aware of the looks that seemed to be suddenly focused just on them, she rose, feeling decidedly unsteady in her unfamiliar boots, and warily settled her hand on top of his.

If he noticed her uncertainty, or cared, he gave no indication. He merely closed his fingers around hers, turned, and pulled her through another gauntlet of tables until they reached the center portion of the huge room where couples were shuffling around in every imaginable dance step, not seeming to care in the least whether they were good at it or not.

She trembled as Russ turned her into his arms, even though he kept a respectable distance between them. Then he swung her into a smooth two-step. "They usually have a better band."

She bit her lip and blinked back the hot sting that burned, threateningly, behind her eyes. He was only dancing with her for the sake of appearances.

But she was supposed to be the one who'd cared about such matters. Not him.

"I think the band sounds fine," she countered huskily.

His gaze looked over her head, beyond her. But his lips twisted. "Probably a lot different than you're used to at that fancy deal your family throws."

She didn't have to look around her to study the laughter and smiling faces that surrounded them and know that the enjoyment the residents of Thunder Canyon found *here* was different than the enjoyment her family's well-vetted guests had at the elegant McFarlane Christmas party. Not that those guests didn't have a good time.

But everything there was timed down to the second. Order reigned supreme beneath the crystal and the caviar, among the black tuxedos and the glittering gowns.

"A lot different," Melanie agreed.

His lips compressed.

"I didn't say better," she added. "I said *different*."

His gaze finally lowered until it focused on her face. "And you're going back there because you can't imagine missing it."

She *could* imagine missing it, just fine, if he'd give

her the slightest reason to do so. "Is there some reason why I should stay here?" Her voice was taut with the tension that held her in its wiry grip.

A shadow came and went in his brown eyes. "You're a grown woman. Suit yourself."

She looked away, staring hard at the lead singer of the band—a grizzled, gray-haired gentleman stomping one boot to the beat, a harmonica in one hand and a beer in the other. But the effort didn't work, and a scalding tear slid past her lashes.

She'd unearthed a suitcase to take with her back to Philadelphia. But she hadn't packed it yet. It sat empty on the floor in her bedroom.

Wasted hopefulness on her part, obviously. Now she'd have to pack up a few things when they returned from the party, because she'd have to be in Bozeman early the next morning to catch her flight.

Another tear escaped.

Russ let out a muffled exclamation and maneuvered her along the crowded dance floor, then off it altogether. She ducked her chin, surreptitiously swiping her hand across her cheek as they rounded the enormous buffet spread. He pushed through a swinging door, and she found them suddenly standing back out in the now empty lobby.

He turned in the claim ticket for their coats, and then he was striding out the door again.

More confused than ever, she slid on her coat and followed. "Russ—"

"We're going home," he said.

She balked. "Maybe I don't want to go back! Maybe I want to eat some of that food you insisted on piling on my plate in there!"

He stopped walking when he reached the town square that was lit by old-fashioned lights atop iron and brick columns and turned on her.

"What are you crying for?"

"What are you angry for?"

They stared at each other, muffled music from the hall curling around them, along with the dancing snowflakes that drifted over their heads.

He finally swore under his breath and propped his hands on the hips of his black jeans, turning away from her. He paced several feet across the brick square, then back again. "What made us think this would work?"

She winced, grateful that he wasn't looking at her. "Everything was working until I, we—"

"Screwed it up. Literally," he muttered and suddenly slammed his fist against the unyielding brick lamppost.

She started, letting out a high gasp that seemed to echo around the square. "Are you crazy?" She reached for his arm, pulling his wrist until she could see his fist.

The knuckles were bloody.

Horrified, she fumbled with the scarf around her hips, worked it free and quickly wadded it up, pressing it around his hand. "You've probably gone and broken something!"

"Better my hand than—" He cut off his terse words. "What if you're pregnant, Melanie?"

Her chilled fingers shook as she tried to tie the ends of the scarf together. "Then I'll d-deal with it just like I deal with everything else."

"Yeah, by running away back to your family?"

"Is that what Nola did?" she demanded. "You keep comparing us, but I am *not* her!"

"I know you're not!" he barked back at her. "But you're still going home for that infernal Christmas party tomorrow, aren't you?"

She tugged the knot in the scarf as tight as it would go and stepped away from him, out of the pool of light glowing over them, because standing so close to him muddled her thinking. "What do you want me to say, Russ? Yes. I'm going back for the party."

"Despite everything that's happened between you."

"They're my family!" She propped her hands on her hips. "At least *I'm* trying to focus on what's worthwhile in that relationship. Maintain some contact, even if it's just through the party. What are *you* doing with your family? Ignoring your son. That's what!"

"What do you know about fatherhood?"

"I know the kind of father I *wish* I had!" She swept her shaking hands down the sides of her skirt and yanked the front of her coat together. "And if by, by some twist of fate being a parent is in my near future after all, I know the kind of parent I'd *hope* I will be."

"I won't let another woman take a child from me."

She wanted to sink down onto the ground and weep; instead, she lifted her chin, straightened her shoulders and looked him square in the eye. "And I don't know why you'd believe that I would ever do such a thing. The only thing I've ever quit in my life was working for McFarlane House. I thought all that stuff was my life. My *entire* life. But you know what? It was just a job. I realize now that's all it ever was. And now I'm trying to *make* a life. A new one for me. And how utterly, utterly stupid," her voice cracked, "I've been for letting myself begin to hope that I could find a partner with whom I c-could share that." She leaned up into his face. "Get used to my presence, Russ Chilton, because McFarlane Christmas party or not, Thunder Canyon *is* my home now, and I am here to stay!"

"You had a one-way flight."

She blinked. "What?"

"I saw the notes you left for yourself. It's a one-way flight."

She pinched the bridge of her nose. "So you naturally assumed that I didn't intend to come back?" She dropped her hand. Looked at him. *"Russ."*

He looked pained. "Well, hell, Melanie, what am I supposed to think?"

"I don't know!" She flapped her arms at her side. "The fact is, you're the one who keeps running away from me. I understand perfectly well that I'm not the kind of woman to keep you interested but—"

"What? Where the hell would you get that notion?"

She had some understanding for him punching the lamppost, because she felt like banging her head against it, if only to stop her impetuous tongue. "I don't know. Perhaps your habit of pretty much disappearing from the Hopping H whenever things get…sticky between us."

"I have another ranch to run," he reminded tightly. "And the only thing *sticky* that I'm avoiding is the fact that my loving wife is…was…a—"

"Virgin?" She shoved her hands through her hair, so far out of control that she wouldn't have cared if there had been people still milling around who might have overheard. "I'm sorry! Believe me, if I could go back in time and find some poor Joe to relieve me of that particular state so that things with you would have been better, I would!"

"Better?" His eyebrows shot up, his face nearly apoplectic, even in the dim light. "Sweetheart, if it were better, we'd both still be in comas."

"Then why—" She broke off, flushing deeply.

"Damn," he muttered under his breath. He paced around some more before stopping in front of her. The pink silk scarf trailed from his wounded knuckles across his hip. "Do you know what it does to a man to know that the woman he…he—"

Her heart stopped beating while he seemed to struggle for words.

"—he cares about—"

"You care about me?"

He frowned impatiently. "He *cares* about," he continued doggedly, "chooses him to be her…first? Particularly when she's waited as long as you have? And don't—" he lifted his hand warningly "—don't go dismissing the subject as if it was just coincidence that you had never had a lover before. That it was your lifestyle, your focus on your career. You're thirty damn years old, honey. And I've seen you in action. If you want something, you go for it. Period. End of story."

She flushed. Did he really see her that way?

The thought was oddly exhilarating.

"But that was obviously something you *never* went for. So, yeah. I can't help but wonder why. Why me? Why now? Forget the fact that we're married on paper. Choosing me as a husband might have been a matter of convenience, but choosing me as your first lover was not, and we both know it!" His jaw centered again. His voice lowered. "Why me, Melanie?"

Her eyes flooded. "I thought there was something

about me that pushed you away. N-not just my red hair. Or what you consider my…Eastern ways. But something inside *me*."

His low, shaking sigh was audible despite the open air, and somehow, she found herself backed against the lamppost, his arms braced above her head, seeming to surround her with his warmth. His…everything. "How many times is it going to take before you realize that all you have to do is breathe, and I want you? It was a…manageable problem…before we toddled on down to Vegas. It was an increasingly inconvenient problem when we got back here during those first few weeks, working side-by-side the way we were. But now—" he lowered his silk-wrapped hand and thumbed away the tears she couldn't seem to stem on her own "—now it is impossible. I want you. Morning. Noon. Night. Anywhere. Everywhere. Get it? But we agreed. Six months, and it would be over. A simple division of property and we'd move on."

"You should have just agreed to my original proposition," she said shakily. "Our marrying for real has only made things more complicated."

He grimaced. "Darlin', the way I feel about you doesn't have squat to do with that piece of legality we signed, or the acreage of the Hopping H I want."

She stared up at him. "What—"

"I'm in love with you. Okay?" He sounded none too happy about it. "So would you please answer my bloody question? Why *me?*"

She exhaled slowly, hardly daring to believe she'd heard right. "You…love me." She moistened her lips. "S-since when?"

His frown grew even blacker. "I don't know. What does it matter since when? Since the time you cried over spilling that drawer. Since you looked your brother in the face and stood up to him. Since you held out a container of worms and smiled up at me and everything that was wrong in my life didn't seem so wrong, after all."

Her vision blurred all over again. "I'm not a crier," she said thickly, wiping her cheeks.

"Yeah," he countered, pulling her hands away and lowering his head to brush away the tears with his lips. "You're not weak. You're not incompetent. You're one of the hardest workers I've ever met. Definitely the most beautiful. And you *are* a crier."

"Russ?"

His mouth hovered over hers. "Yeah?"

She slipped her arms around his neck and looked up into his face. "I love you, too. That's the only reason why *you*." A snowflake landed on his eyelash and she gently brushed it away. "I certainly didn't plan it. But I can't deny it anymore. I don't *want* to deny it anymore."

He covered her mouth with his, kissing her deeply. Thoroughly. Despite the fact that they were there right in the center of town where anyone could come across them exhibiting such wanton behavior.

She didn't care in the least.

But finally, Russ dragged her arms from around his neck, and he looked up at the snowflakes that were falling with more insistence. "No truck cab this time," he warned, as he led her from the square and across to where he'd wedged his ancient orange truck in that narrow slot. She had to slide across the seat from the driver's side, even, because there was not enough room for her to open the door on the other side. "I mean it, Melanie," he said as he climbed in beside her. "So don't tempt me."

Her smile was shaky. "Okay."

He gave her a long, sideways look. "You're still breathing, honey."

She felt as if she were nearly panting. "Just take us home."

The corner of his lips tilted. "Now you're talking." He cranked the engine to life, backed out of the parking slot and gunned the motor practically to the floor when they left the edges of town behind.

"I think you made that drive in record time," she murmured later, when he parked behind the kitchen and swept her across the short snowy distance into the house.

"That may not be the only speed record," he warned with a wry laugh as he herded her through the house, up the steps and into her bedroom where he stopped short.

"You made the bed."

"I often do," she murmured, sliding her arms around his neck, pressing her needy body tight up against him. "Did you think I *never* did any kind of housework?"

He swept his hands down her spine, curved over her rear through the softly crinkled fabric of her skirt, and lifted her right off her feet. "Mebbe."

She laughed softly when he tumbled her onto her back in the middle of the big sleigh bed. "It's not my favorite thing to do," she admitted, "but the more I learn how to manage everything, the easier it is to keep up with it."

"Well." His mouth found her neck and she sucked in a hard breath of delight. "Now that we're here," he worked his hand beneath the hem of her shirt to deftly free the clasp of her bra, "like this, I can admit that the rapid speed of your learning curve is definitely a sweet surprise."

"Sweet?" Emboldened by the glint in his eyes, by the fresh knowledge that she wasn't alone in her emotions after all, she wriggled out of her shirt and pushed him onto his back. "I'm still going to open this place as a guest ranch," she warned. "*And* it'll be the most popular destination of its kind in the area."

Between his thick lashes, his brown eyes glowed almost golden as they focused hard on her. "I wouldn't expect anything else, darlin'. *I'm* still going to be a rancher, and do everything I can to keep this town's progress from getting completely out of control."

"I thought you wanted to stop the progress completely."

He grabbed her waist and neatly flipped her beneath him, trapping her oh so gently with the intent in his eyes. "Then that would mean me stopping you." He threaded his fingers through her hair. "And I never want to see anything, or anyone, ever stop you, Mrs. Chilton."

Her eyes went damp again, and he smiled slightly as he leaned over her and captured her mouth in his.

Chapter Seventeen

Russ rose early the next morning, dragging his exhausted, satiated body out of Melanie's bed only to nearly trip over the empty suitcase sitting at the foot of it.

She was snuggled deep into the mattress, her glowing, tousled hair barely visible above the quilt, and he stared at her for a long while, still trying to adjust to the deep satisfaction that filled what had been empty inside him for so very long.

Careful not to wake her, he pulled on his jeans and padded downstairs, where he realized the snow hadn't just continued drifting through the night.

It had fallen with a vengeance.

Through the windows, he could see the mountainous drifts piled high around and onto the porch. He flipped on the light switch and was glad to see they hadn't lost electricity.

With so much snow, that was a minor miracle.

He stuck a match into the fireplace and got the kindling going, then went into the kitchen and got a pot of coffee going for him, and hot water for her tea.

He found some frozen biscuits in her mammoth-sized freezer, and rooted around until he unearthed a package of frozen sausage, too. The coffee was ready by the time they were both defrosted, and it was only minutes after that, that he had a cast-iron pan full of sausage and gravy started.

But the activities weren't enough to keep his mind off the woman upstairs.

Or the heavy, old-fashioned rotary phone sitting on her desk.

Even after he'd pulled the biscuits out of the oven, cursing when he managed to singe one of his scraped knuckles on the oven door, and had consumed a fair share of the biscuits and gravy, that phone kept beckoning him.

He finally went in and sat at the desk. Why was it so damned hard?

"Just dial the number, Russ." Melanie spoke from the staircase.

He looked over at her as she slowly descended. She'd pulled on a navy-blue flannel shirt that he distinctly, easily remembered as being his, and it hung down around her long, bare thighs. "It'll be all right. I know it will." She smiled softly as she padded, barefoot, past him, stopping momentarily at the sight of the snow outside. "Oh. My."

"You wouldn't have made it to the airport this morning, even if you'd have tried."

"Fortunately, I cancelled my flight reservations already."

He didn't think there was anything more she could do to grab his heart. He was wrong. "When?"

"While you were sleeping. I called my parents, too. They know I won't be there tonight."

"I can imagine how well that went over."

She lifted her shoulder, looking surprisingly calm. "I also promised that we'd visit another time. On our terms. They are my family, Russ. For better or worse."

"*We'd* visit." He grinned slightly. "Bet they'll love that."

"I love *you*. So they'll adjust."

He had to clear his throat suddenly. "Well. Visiting is fine, eventually. For now, consider us snowed in for a day or two."

She slanted a look his direction. "How…intriguing." Then, when she evidently recognized the way his breathing turned a little ragged at the prospect, she smiled again and headed past him into the kitchen.

And he'd thought she was dangerous *before*.

He shook the bemusement from his head and snatched up the phone before he could reason his way out of it again. Remembering the number was no problem. It was permanently engraved inside his brain.

Nola answered.

And for the first time in forever, he realized the sound of her voice had no effect on him. Whether that was Melanie's doing, or time, he didn't know. Didn't care.

It was just a freeing relief.

"Nola. It's Russ. I want to speak with Ryan."

ALLISON LEIGH   237

"Oh." A wealth of surprise sounded in that one word. "Well, he's not here right now. He's out with Boyd."

The stepfather.

"They're picking out a Christmas tree," she went on. "Is everything all right?"

"Yeah. I just want to talk to Ryan. It's been too long."

She was silent for a long moment. "We agreed that it was for the best, Russ."

"I was wrong."

"But we don't want to confuse him."

"I'm his father. There's no confusion about that."

She made a soft sound.

He sat forward, pressing his forehead to his palm. "I've let this go on too long, Nola. He's my son. He has a place in my life. And I should have a place in his. I never fought you in court, Nola, but I will if I have to. You know I've got good reason."

She exhaled. "You haven't changed at all, have you?"

Melanie appeared beside him and ran her hand along his shoulders, stopping to rest on the nape of his neck.

"Yeah, I have," he countered quietly. "Tell Ryan that I called and ask him to call me back." He reeled off Melanie's phone number. "Please," he tacked on out of courtesy if nothing else.

Melanie's fingers slid through his hair. She leaned over him, pressing her lips silently to his head.

He slid his hand around her waist, finding nothing but gloriously smooth, bare skin beneath the shirt.

"All right." Reluctance was still evident in Nola's eventual agreement.

"Thanks." He started to hang up. "Oh. I hope you and Boyd have a Merry Christmas."

"Merry Christmas," she returned, sounding surprised.

He hung up.

"Ryan will call you back," Melanie assured.

He dragged his hand up her back and pulled her down onto his lap. "If he doesn't?" He fiddled with the buttons holding the shirt closed, and one by one they came undone.

She looked up at him, her heart as nakedly bare in her eyes as her beautiful body was. "Then we'll go to Boston," she whispered, and smiled slightly. "At least I know a little hotel where we can stay. I might be able to swing a good rate."

"As long as the bed is wide enough for your antics, I'm happy."

She flushed.

He laughed and suddenly set her on her feet, giving her shapely derriere a swat. "Come on. It's Christmas Eve and you need a tree."

"We can't drive to town and find a tree lot in *that* snow."

He shook his head. "Darlin', this is Thunder Canyon and we both live on ranches. Who needs a tree lot?"

And so they spent the afternoon romping in the snow with two horses, finding a suitable fir tree that he chopped down with an axe and dragged back to the house by a rope tied to his saddle.

He rigged the tree up in the great room near the fireplace and showed her how to make popping corn and string it to hang around the branches.

But still the phone didn't ring.

Not that evening, which they spent by the fire, making love under the fragrant tree. Nor the next morning, which they spent making love in Melanie's wide bed.

But around noon, just when he figured he might collapse from exhaustion, they heard the phone jangle. Melanie's eyes went wide and she raced out of the kitchen, where they were trying to throw together some sandwiches, and snatched up the telephone.

Russ followed more slowly, struggling with the anxiety inside him. But one look at Melanie's face and he knew it wasn't Ryan on the other end.

She held out the telephone. "It's Grant."

And just that quickly, Russ remembered the wedding and snatched up the phone. "Grant. Hell, man, I'm sorry. I—"

"For what? Bolting outta the ball the other night? I figured you must've had some good reason. Aren't you guys snowed in, too?"

"Yeah."

Grant chuckled. "Steph's fit to be tied. We've been trying to dig out for six hours, at least. Needless to say, the ceremony in town is cancelled. But do you think you and Melanie could get by here sometime this afternoon to be our witnesses? I think we'll have plowed through to the highway enough that the preacher can get out here to Clifton's Pride."

"You want to hold the ceremony there?"

"Yeah. Why not? Our families are already here. Steph *is* going to be my wife by the end of this day, one way or another. So, what do you think? Can you make it? I can't get married without my oldest friend standing up for me."

"We'll ride if we have to," Russ promised. "But we'll

be there." He hung up. Eyed his wife. "Stop breathing and distracting me. We've got a wedding to go to."

Her brows shot up, but she gathered her equilibrium quickly. "Will we really have to ride?"

"We might. At least over to the J. I've got a snowmobile that'll make the trip quicker." He gave her a look. "But it's a fair piece, even on a good day. So if you're not—"

She made a face. "Don't even suggest that." She headed for the stairs and seemed to dance her way up them. "I'm going to take a shower," she told him, looking over her shoulder. "And *no,* that isn't an invitation to join me this time. So just keep your distance, or it will be hours before we make it to Clifton's Pride." Even at that distance, he could see the sparkle in her eyes and then she was out of sight.

The phone jangled beneath his hand again and he picked it up. "Two hours," he said. "Definitely no more than three."

"Dad?"

The air inside him left in one big whoosh. He sank down onto the chair. "Hey, Ry. Merry Christmas."

"Yeah." His boy still sounded very much the same. "You, too. I, uh, I got a really cool game system with the money you sent for my last birthday. I meant to call and tell you, but…" His voice trailed off.

"That's okay." Russ pinched his eyes shut and followed Melanie's style. He went for broke. "So, I've missed you a lot, bucko. I thought maybe you might want to come and visit. You know. For a few days or something."

"I got spring break from school in March. Two weeks. Is there still snow there, then?"

Two entire weeks? Nola had never allowed anything longer than a three-day weekend. "Usually."

"Probably can't fish, huh?" He could hear the hesitancy in his son's voice.

He shook his head. Had to clear his throat. "Last time you were here, you didn't seem to want to fish anymore."

"Yeah, but that was, like, a long time ago. So? What's the water like in March?"

"There's a spot here where we can always fish, Ryan."

"Cool. I'll tell Mom. She'll be glad."

Russ highly doubted that. But then maybe Nola had changed some in the intervening years, too.

"Then I won't have to go to the camp she usually sends me to over break," Ryan said.

Nola sent him to *camp?* That was definitely a new one. And if Ryan thought visiting Russ was better than a camp, he wasn't going to turn up his nose at the opportunity, regardless of Ryan's motivation. "So, what are you doing for the Christmas holiday?"

"Going to Boyd's parents'," Ryan said. "In Florida. We leave tonight."

"Thought you called him dad," Russ murmured.

"Sometimes. Mom said it's okay. It is, isn't it?"

When Ryan had been seven, he hadn't thought to ask such a thing. Maybe his voice didn't sound any older, but obviously he was. "It's okay."

"Sweet. Well, I gotta get going. I'm gonna see my best friend before we go to Florida. What're you doing today?"

"I'm going to see *my* best friend get married."

"Oh, yeah? Cool."

"I also got married recently."

"Seriously?" Ryan laughed a little. "Mom'll be surprised. She says you'd never get married again. That you weren't cut out for it."

"Times change."

"What's her name?"

"Melanie."

"She pretty?"

Russ looked over to the staircase. Melanie wasn't standing there at the moment, but he knew he'd forever see her in his mind's eye as if she were. "Beautiful."

"Well, that's good, 'cause you don't want to be having ugly babies." Ryan's voice dropped. "My friend Zach's little sister is ug-ul-ee."

Russ laughed slightly. "Wouldn't let Zach or his family hear you say that."

"Prob'ly not," Ryan agreed. "So I'll see you in March, right? You, um, you won't forget?"

Russ closed his eyes again. "I won't forget, Ryan. I've never forgotten."

"Well, yeah. I guessed that, cause of all the cards and money you keep sending. Mom's not real happy about that, but Boyd just tells her to keep her mouth shut."

Interesting. Maybe Boyd wasn't such a bad guy after all.

"I'll get the plane tickets in the next week or so," Russ said. "And send them to you. How does that sound?"

"Cool. Oh, jeez. Mom's looking for me. I haven't packed my suitcase yet."

"Then you'd better go. I'll talk with you soon. Okay?"

"Yeah. Sure. Later—"

"Ryan."

"Yeah?"

"I love you, son."

"Love you, too, Dad."

And then Russ was left with nothing but a dial tone.

He slowly hung up the phone. Pushed to his feet and headed for the stairs, stopping at the fireplace for a moment as he went. How long would he have gone on without calling his son if it weren't for Melanie?

It didn't bear thinking about.

He went into his room at the end of the hall and found the prenuptial napkin still laying where he'd left it.

He grabbed it and went back down the hall. Outside the bathroom door he could hear the rush of the shower, and he went inside.

"Russ!" Her eyebrows shot up when pulled aside the shower curtain. "I *warned* you!"

"We've got an hour to spare." He held up the tattered napkin and her gaze sobered. She pushed her soaked hair away from her forehead and she turned off the water, reaching for the towel that she wrapped around herself.

That was okay with him. The towel wasn't going to last long. "I want to make a new agreement."

She pressed her lips together. "O-okay. What, um, what exactly do you want it to say?"

He pulled the long match he'd taken from the box by the fireplace and scratched the end against the wall. The tip sparked and turned to flame. He held it against the edge of the napkin and it immediately caught, licking greedily through the thin paper.

He dropped it in the sink where it burned harmlessly to ash, and he blew out the long match and dropped it on top of the tiny remains. Then he turned to face Melanie.

A woman who was changing his life, whether he'd wanted her to or not.

He lifted her hand up to his lips where he kissed the narrow gold wedding ring circling her finger. "The soonest the jeweler opens after Christmas, we're going to get you a decent ring."

She closed her hand into a fist. "I've become rather attached to this one."

"Sure. Particularly when you're washing the green tinge away from your skin." He pulled her close. "Ryan called."

"Oh." Her smile was tremulous. "*Oh.* I'm so happy for you."

"For us."

"For us," she agreed softly. Then smiled all over again. "You see? I told you."

"So you did. And now I'm telling you. You'll have a new ring. One that's going to last you for a long, long time."

Her gaze softened. "Russ."

"And our new agreement only has to say one thing. 'Til death do us part."

Melanie swallowed, staring into his very serious brown eyes. "I…see. That's going to be a very, very, *very* long time, then."

"That's my hope, Mrs. Chilton."

Melanie tilted her lips toward him, everything inside her melting with joy. "Where do I sign, Mr. Chilton?"

He pressed their joined hands to the center of his chest where she could feel his heart beating. Steadily. Surely. For her. For them. For the life she could finally believe that they would have together.

"You already have," he said, sounding deeply contented with that fact. "You already have."

Epilogue

"They look happy, don't they?" Steph murmured into Grant's ear as they swayed to the music playing in the resort's lounge.

"Which *they* are we talking about?" Grant was more interested in the woman he'd made his wife just six days earlier in the living room at Clifton's Pride than he was in the guests crowded into the lounge for the New Year's Eve celebration. "More importantly, are *you* happy?"

Steph wound her arms around his neck. "Blissfully," she assured. "But I *was* referring to Melanie and Russ. They can't seem to keep their eyes or their hands off each other."

That seemed to be pretty much the case with all the couples there as far as Grant could tell. And he was no exception. He'd never been one to avoid a good party, but he'd be perfectly happy to see the last of this one, just so he could get back home with his bride.

"Did you see Mia's mother? Her birth mother, I mean?"

Grant nodded, looking over Steph's head at the woman in question. It was easy to see where Mia had inherited her beauty, because Janelle Josephson had plenty of it to spare. She was also unexpectedly nice. "I heard her talking to Melanie earlier. She's looking for investment opportunities."

Steph swayed against him. "I don't think Melanie's looking for a business partner."

He didn't think so, either. He was just glad that the woman would undoubtedly be sending plenty of her well-heeled friends toward Thunder Canyon for their next vacation. "You're driving me insane, you know," he murmured against her ear.

"I hope so," she murmured right back. "You know, when we were freshening up earlier, Allaire told me she's pregnant. And Shandie hasn't said anything, but I'll bet you she makes an announcement really soon, too."

"Dax'll be happy. He's already wound around Kayla's little finger." Shandie's daughter from her first marriage was quite the little imp. And her stepdaddy adored her as much as he adored Shandie. "D.J. asked Dax to come work with him at the Rib Shack."

Steph pulled back her head, looking surprised.

"Hey, sweetheart. You're not the only one with an ear to the grapevine."

"What'd he say?"

"No. But I think he was still glad that D.J. had asked." He lifted his chin. "Look at 'em over there talking."

Steph craned her head around. "They don't look like they want to pummel each other."

"Exactly." Now that the Traub brothers both were finally matched with their perfect mates, maybe they'd put their differences to rest once and for all. Grant slid his hand down his wife's silky arm, catching her fingers with his. "Are you *sure* you want to stay until the bitter end of this thing?"

She laughed softly. "You're the host, remember?"

He swore softly. "Sometimes I'd just rather have a party of two."

"Soon enough," she soothed, running her fingers through his hair.

"All right, all right. Break it up." Matt and Marlon Cates came up beside them and tugged at Steph until they succeeded in pulling her out of Grant's arms. "We've just spent the worst few days trying to get back to Thunder Canyon from school, and when we get here, all the pretty women are taken," Matt complained.

Grant looked over at their older brothers. Mitch had his arm around Lizbeth, and Marshall was ignoring everyone in favor of his black-haired wife, Mia. No help from that quarter, obviously.

"Can't you find your own women?" Grant challenged the younger men.

Marlon grinned wickedly. "Well, we did meet these two beautiful girls on our way here…"

"Hey," Lizbeth's voice rose above the music. "Look. It's nearly midnight!"

Suddenly, all around them, people were shouting out the countdown.

"Four. Three. Two. One! Happy New Year!"

Grant ignored the youngest Cates boys and pulled his wife into his arms, kissing her, as streamers and confetti exploded over their heads, right on time, just as he'd arranged.

And then there was more laughing and more kissing and his wait staff was doing a reasonable job of filling champagne glasses for the horde crowded into the lounge.

When he could see that everyone had a glass, Grant lifted his high, holding Steph tight to his side. "Here's a toast to the best damn year Thunder Canyon has ever seen."

A ripple of cheers followed.

"Not exactly," Russ countered, eyeing Grant across the couples between them with a smile playing around his lips. "Here's to the future," he countered. "And the best damn years that Thunder Canyon will *ever* see."

And at that, the room erupted.

Grant watched Russ long enough to see his old friend swing Melanie around in a circle and toss back his head in the kind of laughter he hadn't seen in a long, long time.

Grant hooked his own wife under his arm, and he nodded, satisfied.

Russ was right.

The best years *were* yet to come.

* * * * *

Silhouette® Desire

When Kimberley Blackstone's father is presumed dead, Kimberley is required to take over the helm of Blackstone Diamonds. She has to work closely with her ex, Ric Perrini, to battle not only the press, but also the fierce attraction still sizzling between them. Does Ric feel the same...or is it the power her share of Blackstone Diamonds will provide him as he battles for boardroom supremacy.

Look for

VOWS & A VENGEFUL GROOM

by

BRONWYN JAMESON

Available January wherever you buy books

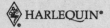

REQUEST YOUR FREE BOOKS!
2 FREE NOVELS PLUS 2 FREE GIFTS!

SPECIAL EDITION®
Life, Love and Family!

YES! Please send me 2 FREE Silhouette Special Edition® novels and my 2 FREE gifts. After receiving them, if I don't wish to receive any more books, I can return the shipping statement marked "cancel." If I don't cancel, I will receive 6 brand-new novels every month and be billed just $4.24 per book in the U.S., or $4.99 per book in Canada, plus 25¢ shipping and handling per book and applicable taxes, if any*. That's a savings of at least 15% off the cover price! I understand that accepting the 2 free books and gifts places me under no obligation to buy anything. I can always return a shipment and cancel at any time. Even if I never buy another book from Silhouette, the two free books and gifts are mine to keep forever.

235 SDN EEYU 335 SDN EEY6

Name _____ (PLEASE PRINT)

Address _____ Apt. _____

City _____ State/Prov. _____ Zip/Postal Code _____

Signature (if under 18, a parent or guardian must sign)

Mail to the **Silhouette Reader Service™:**
IN U.S.A.: P.O. Box 1867, Buffalo, NY 14240-1867
IN CANADA: P.O. Box 609, Fort Erie, Ontario L2A 5X3

Not valid to current Silhouette Special Edition subscribers.

Want to try two free books from another line?
Call 1-800-873-8635 or visit www.morefreebooks.com.

* Terms and prices subject to change without notice. NY residents add applicable sales tax. Canadian residents will be charged applicable provincial taxes and GST. This offer is limited to one order per household. All orders subject to approval. Credit or debit balances in a customer's account(s) may be offset by any other outstanding balance owed by or to the customer. Please allow 4 to 6 weeks for delivery.

Your Privacy: Silhouette is committed to protecting your privacy. Our Privacy Policy is available online at www.eHarlequin.com or upon request from the Reader Service. From time to time we make our lists of customers available to reputable firms who may have a product or service of interest to you. If you would prefer we not share your name and address, please check here. ☐

Silhouette

nocturne™

Jachin Black always knew he was an outcast.
Not only was he a vampire, he was a vampire
banished from the Sanguinas society. Jachin, forced
to survive among mortals, is determined to buy
his way back into the clan one day.

Ariel Swanson, debut author of a vampire novel, could
be the ticket he needs to get revenge and take his
rightful place among the Sanguinas again. However,
the unsuspecting mortal woman has no idea of the
dark and sensual path she will be forced to travel.

Look for

RESURRECTION: THE BEGINNING

by

PATRICE MICHELLE

Available January 2008 wherever you buy books.

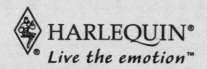

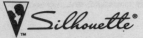
TM **Silhouette**®

COMING NEXT MONTH